Inte_____on

by

C.S. Barnes

Margaret –

I hope you enjoy this!

All love –

Barnes

X.

A note from the narrator

When I was four years and nine months old, it occurred to me that I might be different. Not in the overtly self-conscious way that most people will feel at one time or another; I was a child, after all. But on those first taster days of school I already didn't like the other children; I didn't feel challenged by the lessons; I didn't miss my mum. They're relatively small things, but I've come to think of them as building blocks – strong foundations for slightly larger issues. For instance, when I was eight years and six months old, I squeezed the life out of our family cat. My mother told me that it wasn't my fault. Poppy was old, and it certainly wasn't anything that I had done. I don't think she understood what I was trying to tell her.

To begin with it was a passing thought, a curiosity I only pursued due to the absence of company. By ten years and two months of age, my father had become so preoccupied with beating my mother – and my mother so preoccupied with covering her bruises with make-up – that they barely noticed what their little girl was occupying herself with. In fact, the behaviour went so unnoticed that I managed to convince myself that it was quite normal; that working out the amount of weed killer required to annihilate a catalogue of household animals was a perfectly acceptable pastime for any above-average-intelligence preadolescent. Regrettably, despite my desire to normalise it, my growing intelligence hindered my adoption of that belief with any real conviction. The first time my mother picked a pungent carcass – it was a swallow, or some other bird of a similar size – from my windowsill and deposited it in the outside rubbish bin, I knew that I was crossing some lines.

'I just found it,' I had told her. 'I wondered how long it would take to change.'

Decompose, I meant, and I think she knew. But nothing more was ever said on the matter. That was my first real mistake. Although, the fish in the freezer incident was a childish error on my part, too, but we'll come to that later.

When fully-fledged adolescence arrived, the household in which I lived transformed into your average miserable family. Miserable because alcohol is a depressant, not a mood lifter – a reality that my father insisted on testing and verifying for himself on a daily basis. Everyone in our local Accident and Emergency Department was on a first name basis with my mother by the time I was eleven years and eight months old. Through my ritualistic attendance of the hospital's visiting hour to see her, they soon came to be on a first name basis with me too.

For a while it was convenient to believe that my mother was just clumsy; that doors, floors, and other miscellaneous items around the house were somehow conspiring against her. However, when a boy at my secondary school asked an allegedly innocent question about my father's behaviour towards my mother – 'Like, does your dad do it a lot or…?' – I discovered that not everyone was capable of ignoring it as well as me. A nervous laugh moved in a Mexican wave around the classroom, and then I thumped the boy in the face. A bloody mess escaped from his nose as he dabbed away tears. I was thoroughly impressed. My mother, less so.

'We don't use violence; it doesn't fix problems,' she had said.

'So why does Dad do it?'

We didn't talk for a week after that. She broke her vow of silence, just once, to inform me that my father was cleaning out the fish pond. She muttered something about dead fish and contaminated water and then turned back to the task at hand: ironing my father's best white shirt ahead of his evening with friends. I asked if the water smelt like bleach, but she didn't answer. I can't remember whether it was her silence or something else altogether, but that week I heard everything for the first time. It seemed my ears had become attuned to the sounds of my father's after-hours activities. And apparently once you tune into that frequency, you can never turn it off.

The only time my mother and father presented a truly united front was in their efforts to hide the injuries that followed, yet there were times when they couldn't even manage that. One morning stands out in particular; their antics from the previous evening had left my mother's right hand entirely useless. This was something my father regretted when his breakfast was served fifteen minutes late. Each offer of assistance from me was greeted by 'she can manage'. Losing patience, he squashed my fifth offer of help. The grip of his fingers around my wrist was quickly followed by a twist, and then a grinding sensation.

'You get that bloody hand off her.'

It was my mother's first and only intervention.

That evening I felt the front leg of a stray cat crack inside my hand. I realised then that his angle hadn't been right at all, not if he'd wanted to break a bone.

On reflection, it could be considered a perverse achievement that we lived like this for so long. But times change and I, as most children do, eventually had to depart for greener pastures. The beatings worsened after I left for university. My mother never told me, explicitly, but she never really needed to. My early video chats with her soon disintegrated into half-video, half-darkness; while my face was suspended in the corner of my laptop screen, the space that hers should occupy remained black. Given that she never mentioned it, I assumed that I wasn't expected to either. With this home-life situation a secondary concern now, my main problem became how to correctly perform an autopsy on a pig – a primary concern for most biology students at university, and one that I took to with disproportionate excitement. In this new setting, the animal-based experiments that I had so frequently performed at home became something worth sharing, with a room full of people no less, all of whom were up to their elbows in entrails themselves.

My fellow students would animate carcasses – using one hand to manipulate the mouth of a long-dead animal while providing an amusing voice-over for the creature – and smuggle organs into each other's work spaces in a manner that I found refreshing, encouraging even. The interactions with these new associates helped me to grow and explore myself in a way that I was told I should at university. One classmate – Angela Straven – even shared her experiences with formaldehyde and methanol over two bottles of wine and a girls' night, and from this the preservation of my experiments was born and the subsequent storage of them as well. It all went a long way towards normalising my behaviour, although it's possible that wasn't a good thing.

On an irregular basis I was lured away from my student life of beans on toast, animal dissections, and *Friends* reruns. My mother was always pleased, or relieved, to have me home, while my father often greeted me with a notable lack of interest – that is, of course, on the few occasions when he felt moved enough to greet me at all. If nothing else, these visits home reminded me of precisely why I had abandoned the house and its misfit occupants in the first place, so perhaps, in that sense, they served a purpose.

Our family history may make for a surprising read, I suppose, for anyone viewing it from an external angle. We managed. It was our very own version of normality. The most surprising element, in fact, is not the abuse and the subsequent damage that it caused at all. The most surprising thing, I think, is that one of us didn't die sooner.

Chapter one

We were dropped back into the dysfunctional dynamics of family life at the end of my second year of university, when I reluctantly returned home for the summer months. A complication with contracts – thanks to my would-be housemates – meant that keeping away for the holidays was not an option that year. On the afternoon of my arrival, my mother's arm was already tucked away in a sling which disappeared after a day or two; I had just escaped an outburst. Beyond that everything was average, unchanged. After my first evening in my own bed, my first morning was made up of dead air between my father and me; I made tea in the kitchen as he tried to read his morning paper. He tutted, shuffled the pages. Something was irking him but I didn't want to ask what. He left the house without saying a word and that's when my mother appeared; bright-eyed and unexpectedly chirpy, she set about making breakfast with an unnecessary smile on her face. My deadpan expression – somewhere between amused and bemused – felt misfit.

'Are you okay, love?' my mother asked, back to me, buttering toast.

'Of course,' I lied. I wasn't okay but I was unsure of why.

We shared a quiet breakfast of toast and too-strong tea while my mother enquired about my plans for the day – I had none – and I toyed with the idea of asking what hers were. It had never crossed my mind what my mother did all day: how she filled the time, what a normal Tuesday might be. Tuesdays were cleaning days, as I later discovered.

'Will the Hoover disturb you?'

My head was firmly wedged inside JG Ballard's *Crash*.

'Gillian?' She sounded nervous; how she must sound when she talks to my father in similar circumstances, I thought.

'Sorry?'

'The Hoover.'

'Oh.' I shook my head. 'That's fine, it won't disturb me.'

After this, my Stepford mother reappeared to clean corners of the house that had long been forgotten and were now only inspected by her.

'There are some places the Hoover just can't reach,' she said, scrubbing away.

I couldn't offer a complementary response and so I opted for a subject change. 'What time will Dad be home?'

My mother was on her knees, angled in such a way that I could only see her backside rising and dipping intermittently, and an elbow jutting out in a determined beat as she rubbed at something in the corner of the living room.

'The shop closes at half past five now, so he should be home by six because Tuesday isn't a pub night. I don't know when dinner will be,' she added, pre-empting my next query.

I felt she had given me more information than I needed, like she was providing me with tips for surviving Tuesdays. Would I get these every day?

My mother was right about the timing. At six on the dot, my father wandered into the house and stuck his head into the kitchen to deliver a curt nod of 'Hello' to my mother and a stare of disapproval to me. He smelt of raw meat; the odour of a butcher that I had come to exclusively associate with him.

This clockwork running of the house appeared common practice for them. Everything was timed down to the minute from my father showering the work-day off himself, right through to my mother setting the Sky box to record her soaps – 'So we can skip through the adverts,' she said, as though this were an activity I was expected to partake in. They – we – even ate dinner together.

'Could you pass the salt?' I asked anyone.

'You don't need salt,' my father replied.

Nevertheless my mother passed the shaker; my father passed her a disapproving look. Tuesdays may have been cleaning days but in my first four days of being at home, cleaning was all I saw my mother do. It appeared as a compulsion for her, as if something important depended on clean corners and properly swept floors. Late one Friday afternoon – when the house was a clinical level of clean after a week of bleach and buffing – my mother wandered upstairs and through my open doorway. The time had come; we were going to have a chat.

She found me lying down in my room – another unchanged element of the house; it still held a single bed, still boasted pink walls. I was poring over the pages of a book with feigned concentration.

'Do you have a minute, love?'

'What do you need?'

'I just thought we could have a little chat.'

I shook away the beginnings of a frown. 'About?'

'Oh, anything.' She edged closer to my bed, making the journey in small movements, as if hoping that I wouldn't see how close she now was. 'How's university going?'

Eternal Sunshine of the Spotless Mind. 2004. Jim Carrey. 'Constantly talking isn't necessarily communicating.'

We discussed university, we discussed my plans for the summer – again, I had none – and we skirted around the issue of how I felt about being home. Disgruntled, mostly, but that wasn't a feeling that I shared with my mother. Instead I told her it was a change, and I would adapt, as would Dad. She hadn't mentioned my father at all during the conversation but I knew that was the direction in which we would eventually steer things.

'He doesn't mind you being here,' she said, responding to something that I hadn't asked.

'No?'

'No.'

'Geraldine!'

My mother's shoulders bunched up as if trying to shield her from something.

'Dinner!'

It wasn't a question so much as a command. My mother shot me a look – almost a grimace that cocked her mouth up at one side. With a shrug she stood and paced to my doorway, asking on the way: 'What would you like for dinner, love?'

'I don't care.'

I don't mind, I should have said.

'Woman!' My father launched the word up the stairs like a small grenade; the sound was guttural, aggressive. My mother again flinched at the sound before flashing an uncomfortable smile and moving from the doorway.

The quiet that followed this incident was deceptive. When I ventured downstairs a short while later, I heard the throaty laugh of my father drifting out of the living room. I crept past the doorway and made for the kitchen where I discovered, resting in the corner of the room, a complete dinner slumped on top of a ruined plate that had been cracked into five neat pieces. In the opposing corner there stood my mother, trying to settle a tremor as she soaked her hand beneath the cold tap. Despite seeing everything, I couldn't make it all fit.

'Is he having dinner with us?' I asked.

'It was too hot. I should have warned him.'

The Wizard of Oz. 1939. Judy Garland. 'There's no place like home.'

My mother pulled out a chair opposite me but, after a second of deliberation, sat hesitantly on the one next to me instead, as if her first choice was too suggestive of confrontation. With a damp cloth tucked around her injured hand, she was left with no other option but to use only the edge of her fork to chip away at her dinner. It was unexpectedly satisfying to see her struggle.

While my mother tentatively chewed a series of half-mouthfuls, I fell into rearranging my dinner into different patterns across my plate. She eventually noticed.

'Is there something wrong with your food?'

'No, there's something wrong with my family.'

Something flitted over her face; was it disappointment? Surprise? Discomfort?

'Can I speak openly?' I knew this was the proper way to introduce a potentially difficult conversation. I'd heard it said on television.

'I thought you already were.' Her tone was blunt; it didn't fit her at all. But then it softened. 'We hardly have secrets here, love, you can say what you like.'

A problem that I had often experienced was an inability to devote an appropriate amount of consideration to a thought before voicing it. Too little and the thought was clumsy, misshapen; too much and it was clinical, accusatory. Despite having a loose idea of what I wanted to say, there wasn't quite enough time to format it, which is perhaps why it emerged as an emotional blunt force trauma: 'Why didn't you ever try to leave?'

My mother dropped her fork and it bounced off her dinner plate, making for a dramatic gesture. I remained silent, stern, perhaps even parental. 'Do we have to have this conversation, Gillian?'

In my experience it was considered bad form to answer a question with a question, but it didn't seem appropriate to highlight this. Nor did it seem appropriate to suggest that the reason we were having this conversation was because the issue had never been addressed before, and there was only so much extracurricular reading I could do around the so-called battered-woman syndrome before my curiosity called for first-hand research.

'It hasn't always been like this, and you know it,' she started. 'I wouldn't have been stupid enough to marry him if he was already like he is now.'

Perhaps not, but stupid enough to stay with him, I thought.

'We were a good couple once, Gillian.'

There was a long pause then. I wondered whether she was trying the sentence on for size, to see if she could somehow make it fit.

'What changed?' I asked.

'Why is this something we need to talk about?'

'I can always go in there and ask him.'

'He'd beat you black and blue if you did.'

'I'd end up killing him if he tried.'

The answer startled the both of us.

'Don't talk like that, Gillian.'

'Like what?'

'Like violence can fix problems, because it bloody can't.'

'No, violence just creates problems, doesn't it?' I matched her tone, pushing harder than I had during adolescence. She knew what I was asking her; I knew she wouldn't answer. 'Am I the reason you didn't leave?' I considered this a calculated risk. Statistically speaking, I was probably one of several reasons why she hadn't left, but whatever detained her in the house now, it certainly wasn't me. And the longer I spent away from our family, the stronger my desire grew to understand what had broken it.

'Gillian, love, no, of course it wasn't anything to do with you. All of this started long before we'd even decided to have you.' I nodded; she hadn't answered my question. 'Gillian, what is it that you really want to know?'

'Why you're here. Why you don't leave now.'

'This is just life, love. The only way one of us will leave now is in a box.' And at that she returned to the remainder of her dinner.

Inside the sanctuary of my bedroom I perched on my bed and assessed my surroundings. The room hadn't changed in as long as I could remember. The same pink paint, picked out by my mother, occupied the majority of the wall space, bar the occasional stretches of scab where my younger self had sought to peel away the colour. Now, as a twenty-two-year-old woman, I was still confined to a child's bedroom, sleeping on a bed that was dressed up in a duvet cover I hardly even recognised. Opposite the bed there was a desk, the top space of which was dominated by a television so old that there was still a cuboid attached to the back of it.

I allowed myself an indulgent dip into my experiments box. On my return home I'd stashed it inside my wardrobe, but the time had arrived now for me to fall back on it; between you and me, I was surprised that I'd lasted so long. Through the slightly open folds of cardboard I could see a circular, stained-silver lid, but I couldn't decipher which jar it belonged to. With my eyes shut, I wrapped my fingers around the first container that they landed on. The liquid shifted noisily as I retrieved the jar. And there it was, as luck would have it: the rat. The first of my keepsakes.

Before moving home, the contents of the box had reserved shelf space opposite my bed at university, where I could keep an eye on them. Lined up from the oldest – and therefore the favourite – to the most recent, there was a time when I said goodnight to each of them in turn before going to sleep. Claire – a fellow lover of animals and their anatomies who I encountered during my first year – had once gone to the effort of naming them all.

'Where did you even get them from, Gillian?' she asked one night, throwing a jar of small organs between her hands with such enthusiasm that they created something akin to a rattle.

'I sort of put them together myself.'

We hadn't spoken since, although she did throw me the occasional glance, laden with judgement, when our paths crossed on campus. My first real lesson from university was censorship.

Now, turning the container this way and that, I struggled to get the head and the body alongside each other in such a way that I could admire both. It had been four years, but it looked much the same as when I had first dropped both sections into the solution, although its eyes stared back a little duller than they used to. It was once just water, but the animal's decomposition rate put a stop to that. The rat and I had moved along in preservation techniques since then. The cut had been clumsy, jagged, rushed; I remembered my analysis of it particularly well. But I suppose everyone remembers their first.

This quick pull of a memory wasn't as satisfying as a fresh experience but it was the best remedy I could get that evening. I stared into its eyes and lost myself there, until–

'Gillian, I have to–'

My mother entered the room without my even realising it. The jar slipped from between my fingers as she spoke; I pulled in a mouthful of air, as if filling my lungs would somehow soften the oncoming blow. The glass itself collided with the rug rather than the wood, creating a dull thud. She reached; I reached. Her hand grabbed the container before mine was even close. She couldn't help but study the specimen then. The frown lines on her forehead were soon ironed away and replaced with wide eyes.

'I'm interrupting you. I, ah, I'm sorry–'

She settled the jar on the bed as she spoke, as if the duvet might be too hard a surface for it. She stepped back then, three small steps, before speaking again, as if the distance had given her the necessary space to continue.

'I'm going out now. For his beer. I... would you like to come with me, or...?'

I wondered how that sentence could possibly finish. Would you prefer to stay here? Spend some time with your father? Play around with your dead things?

'I'll stay here. I'll keep an eye on him while you're away, shall I? Make sure he doesn't dehydrate, or choke on a ring pull?'

'Oh, Gillian, it's best to just keep out of his way,' she whispered, like she was telling me something that I didn't already know. 'I'll hardly be any time at all, and, well, I wouldn't want there to be any trouble.'

From my bedroom window I watched, waited. The front door slammed, the car engine coughed itself awake, and twenty seconds later I heard heavy footfalls, slowly increasing in volume. My father had just reached the top of the stairs when I pulled my bedroom door closed behind me. His bloodshot eyes tipped back in his head when he saw me, and I wondered who else he had been expecting to find up here. In the seconds of surveillance that followed, I saw that his shirt was buttoned up wrong, his belt only half held together by its buckle, and the bottle of lager in his right hand was half-empty – or half-full, depending on your perspective.

'You're a little undressed, Dad.'

'For what? Slobbing about my own house?'

I didn't correct him. If slobbing was his primary concern then he was well-dressed for the occasion.

'You're the one who should be getting dressed up. Hitting the town, like a normal kid,' he said, leaning heavily on the word 'normal', punctuating the sentence with a rough laugh.

'Nothing about this house is normal.'

There was every chance, I thought, that he either wouldn't hear or wouldn't properly process what I had said. But when his face snapped towards me with a deadpan expression, I knew that neither of those possibilities had come to fruition.

'Nothing about this house is normal?' he repeated, squinting, inspecting the appraisal. He appeared offended by the assessment. Taking an additional step away from the stairs, he moved closer to me.

I could catch fragments of something downstairs. It was Thursday; we had eaten dinner nearly an hour ago, so it must have been either *Coronation Street* or *EastEnders*. I had lost track of the timetable since moving away. Over-dramatised bursts of 'You're not my mother' and 'And what a relief that is' infiltrated our tension. Apparently my father and I were not the only individuals on the cusp of a family squabble.

'What are you doing?' he asked, as if I had been the one to approach him. I glanced down and assessed myself; I didn't appear to be doing anything. 'Don't get smart with me,' he said, as though guessing my reply. 'You waltz in here, like you own the place. Eating our food, leaching off us. Putting thoughts in your mother's head.'

My mouth twitched into a smirk that I didn't even try to suppress.

'Don't you bloody grin.' He paused to swig from his bottle before lowering it back down; it was his first sip since this encounter had started. When he spoke again his voice was level, controlled. 'I'll get you out of here again before you know it,' he said with a newfound measure of confidence, like there were a master plan sitting behind the threat. 'And if you put ideas in her head about leaving, I'll get rid of that problem as well.'

Feelings and their titles often evaded me entirely but there was something – a tug, somewhere in my innards – when he said that.

'Get rid of the problem? Is that me, or her?'

'Think I'll pop her under the patio; chop her up in the shop?' At least I knew which one of us he was referring to now. But the good humour, the obvious enjoyment that went into the retort, was perturbing. He seemed proud. 'Hey, let's bond, kiddo. We can cut her up and feed her to those hungry strays that you've been picking off over the years; it's about time we gave something back to them.'

He extended an arm out to the banister behind him, leaning back against it triumphantly. 'We've all got our bad habits, kid.' He was smug now, chasing the words with another mouthful of alcohol. 'Not so different after all, eh?'

I needed to speak. But nothing was coming out. I couldn't rationalise how we had arrived here; what had made my father so hungry for this, what had made him part with his ammunition so readily?

'You were a mistake, you know?' he started again. 'A rotten mistake that your mother refused to take care of. Didn't agree with abortion, didn't think we could get rid; I reckoned we could, though. Reckoned a good hiding was what she needed.'

If I was pushed, really pushed, to isolate the moment when I lost control, it would be then.

Fact: studies have shown that women are slower to experience rage than men. He moved forward and, driven by biological instinct alone, I retreated. There was something simultaneously familiar yet alien about the way he padded towards me – a semi-tranquillised bear determined to catch its prey. As he made good progress at closing the distance between us, I saw his jaw tighten, eyes twitch, fists clench.'

'Eventually your mother will know what a mistake you were.'

He punctuated his speech by throwing a clenched fist towards me, missing by mere centimetres each time; it was the difference between a drunk offence and a sober defence. My reaction times were quicker than his burning anger, but this only seemed to add force to his feelings. We paced about on the landing, both light-footed with eyes fixed on the other.

Fact: the home is a much more dangerous environment than anywhere else for those living with domestic violence.

Almost out of nowhere a palm collided with my cheek. My teeth clamped down on the inside of my mouth and my saliva became metallic.

'I thought I'd ease you in,' he said, a laugh disturbing his speech. 'You're hardly as

experienced as your mum.'

And then I pushed him; heard the misplaced, unsteady footfalls of a heavyweight drunk tipped off balance, with open hands clambering for something to hold on to.

Fact: while very few women do resort to violence, when they do so it is usually as a response to violence that they have already received from a partner or parent.

He landed awkwardly at the bottom of the stairs. A foot away from his head lay the beer bottle he had been holding; the glass had split into large chunks that were now doused in lager, trying to make an escape from the scene.

Before I had even started down the stairs I knew that he was still breathing. He must have been, otherwise the whole thing would have been too easy, too simple, too straightforward.

Women everywhere would have murdered their unmentionable men had it been this easy.

Fact: it is not a foregone conclusion that someone will die from a broken neck, but it is easier to break the human neck when the muscles around it are relaxed.

The rise and fall of his chest gave the impression of sleep.

It's not uncommon to hear of a household suffering from domestic violence. Nor is it uncommon to find the female members of the household striking back – and that doesn't exclusively refer to the wife either, thankfully. The legal system will throw around 'manslaughter' and 'cumulative rage', perhaps even 'cumulative terror' depending on how much the occasion calls for it. Assuming, that is, that the whole thing isn't just a terrible accident in the home, and in my father's case it may well have been.

I sat four steps above him. He had been unconscious for some thirty seconds.

I couldn't risk him waking up, or my mother coming home, before I'd finished.

Fact: females are inclined towards strangulation. A ligature mark alone is not definitive evidence of this method. And with a soft enough ligature, there will be no mark left behind at all.

Chapter two

I lost twelve minutes just looking at him, eyes unblinking, waiting for something like a punchline. At some point, although I couldn't tell you when exactly, his eyes had opened. I repositioned myself on the stairs, four steps above him again, and noticed that the eyes had settled on me with impressive accuracy. The body lay at a peculiar angle, which I thought would be convincing in line with a fall at least, but simultaneously the whole scene looked staged. Like a red-band film poster for the latest home invasion thriller.

I could almost hear the critics: 'This latest image release from Thompson offers an interesting commentary on contemporary society. The alpha male, murdered in what appears to be his own home; doesn't bode well, does it?'

And then they'd all laugh.

I laughed.

The noise sounded alien.

His eyes had died with a hint of disapproval in them. I couldn't maintain contact with them and so allowed my own eyes to rest somewhere beneath his, like an embarrassed child caught doing something that they shouldn't have done. Kicking their sibling, stealing a cookie, killing something. I was waiting for my reprimand; waiting for him to wake up; waiting for him to tell me just how much I'd fucked up this time.

I laughed again, accidentally, like a belch that I couldn't hold in.

'Have you really died then?'

This scenario had been constructed and reimagined repeatedly. And in amongst the idle planning from my childhood, my adult self had researched, hard, and catered to all options – accidental death, or perhaps manslaughter, pleaded down to self-defence.

I swallowed another laugh.

(Why couldn't I stop laughing?)

I flicked through a bank of reactions, trying to find something appropriate.

Crying was a possibility.

Some sort of hysteria, catatonia, even.

Shock.

(Was this shock?)

An emotional breakdown of a non-specific nature. That's what people did when someone died. You could see it everywhere: *Casualty, Four Weddings and a Funeral,* the lifestyle section of your average women's magazine.

There was an emotional fallout that was noticeably lacking from the experience, though. And I don't just mean the one that I should have been feeling, but rather the one that I always felt. A feeling of fulfilment; a loosening of the stomach muscles and a drop of the shoulders as though taking a deep exhale. There was usually… something. On the surface it seemed like another thing to blame my father for: he hadn't even managed to die in a satisfactory manner. The counterargument, though: I hadn't even managed to kill him properly. I waited – hoped – for some recognition, for my brain to catch up with what my hands had just done, but my nerve endings were miscommunicating the actions – nothing connected, nothing stirred. I waited for my limbic system, the hippocampus, the amygdala, the latter of which should have some part to play given the possibility of incarceration now. I inhaled deeply, feeding my thalamus, but before the neurotransmitters could fire I heard my mother's voice: 'Oh God, Gillian, what have you done? Gillian? Gillian, what happened here? Did you do this, Gillian?'

I felt concerned that she might wear my name out, in the same way that certain words stop looking like words when you write them too many times. But I didn't say that; I didn't say anything.

My mother kicked her way through the collection of carrier bags that had landed around her. She dropped to the floor with a thud heavy enough to damage her knees. She slid herself closer towards us and sat, wedged between my father and the base of the stairs, unsure of who to turn to, unsure of which one of us needed her. I didn't realise, until her fingers landed around my wrist, that she was shaking. She kept quiet, but I knew what she was thinking. What had happened? What had I done? How could this have happened? She'd hardly been gone any time at all. Why wouldn't I answer?

'Gillian!'

I began to hate the sound of my own name.

'Did it really happen, Mum?'

It was tactical, right down to the 'Mum' strategically tagged on at the end. And when she wrapped her arms around my neck and shoulders, leaving me grimacing with the taste of ripe affection in my mouth, I realised it was a tactic worth relying on again in the future.

'We'll fix this, baby, we'll fix this.'

She had never before and has never since referred to me as 'baby'.

I wanted to know what we were going to do, how exactly we were going to fix things –

how far a mother would go to protect her child. But she didn't explain. Instead, she bought herself three minutes of thinking time. We stayed in an unfamiliar embrace. My head rested on her shoulder at an uncomfortable angle, and I felt her fingers stroke at the back of my hair as we rocked. She cooed the occasional 'Ssssh' as we moved, as if I were an infant again.

I watched my father's corpse over her shoulder.

At the end of those precious moments, she concluded: 'We need to call the police.'

Yes, I thought, because that would fix things.

***

'The police, and an ambulance – maybe an ambulance, I don't know, I think it might be too late, too late for a...' She fumbled, as if she'd forgotten the word. 'It was an accident, it all just happened so quickly that I – Christ we just need the police here.' Another pause, this one a fraction longer. I heard her shifting her weight from one foot to the other. 'How long do you think it will take? What should I do until then?'

My mother's half of the conversation came tumbling out from the living room, disguised as white noise now. I couldn't concentrate on her chatter; I was preoccupied with the body that was lying in front of me, its face now covered with a tea towel.

'They'll be here soon, love, not long to wait now.'

Her speech cut through my concentration. She hovered in the doorway as she spoke. 'Gillian, love, do you think you can talk to me now? Explain what happened? I'm going to need to know. I'm going to need to know what I should tell them.' She moved closer to me as she spoke and it occurred to me that she might be about to comfort me, although out of the two of us she was clearly the more agitated one.

'It was an accident,' I started. I thought it was best to try this out on my mother first. 'He lost his temper with me. I don't even know why, I can't think. I only pushed him away.' I didn't have to admit to it, no. But the best lies are inspired by true events. 'I just pushed him. I never thought... I just didn't think, and when I knew he'd fallen–' The further into the explanation I ventured, the more prominent my tears became. My mother shushed me – in that patronising yet maternal way – and pulled me close towards her.

'I went out to get your father something to drink. You stayed upstairs and started to unpack your things. When I got home, he–' She paused for thought.

I pulled away to observe her. A crease had formed between her eyes and two teeth were now tugging on her bottom lip; thinking appeared to be a painful process.

'When I got home he was angry. He said that I'd taken too long and he lost his temper with me, not with you. I was scared, you were in the house and I didn't want it – no, I didn't want you to be involved. So, when he came towards me, to hit me, I pushed him away, and that's when he lost his balance.' She paused again as she finished piecing together this reimagining. 'You heard raised voices and so you stayed out of the way, but when it went quiet that's when you came to see what had happened. Do you understand?'

One point for believability.

One point for feasibility.

Two points for effort.

I had never seen her so controlled.

I nodded in agreement, although I tried to appear tentative before asking: 'Why don't we just tell them the truth?'

It was a potentially dangerous question but still one that I had to ask. If I hadn't, then it would have come to her at a later date, when this was all over and the shock had worn off. I had to ask it because at some point in the future it would occur to her that I hadn't thought telling the truth was even an option; it wasn't, of course, and it never had been, but my mother couldn't know that.

The doorbell rang. Before she moved away from me she threw back: 'Because I can't lose the both of you.'

And for the briefest time I wondered how much of my explanation she believed.

'Thank you for coming,' I heard her say, presumably to the police officers waiting behind the door, hidden from my line of vision. It seemed a strange thing to say, given the circumstances. 'It's been – I can't explain, it all just happened so fast and, God, I can't believe this has happened at all.' My mother's new role: traumatised woman meets accidental murderer.

'Okay, miss, I need you to tell me: is there anyone else here?'

'My daughter. My daughter, yes, just through there.' She opened the door a little further and stepped to the side, allowing the officers a half-view of me, and regrettably an even clearer view of the body on the floor in our hallway.

My inappropriate desire to laugh returned as I watched, but lodged in my throat like a piece of popcorn determined to ruin the best scene of a film.

My mother delivered a comprehensive explanation for the mess that currently occupied the hall, stuttering intermittently throughout, as if that was somehow valid evidence of her shock and bereavement. The officers listened, although one occasionally shifted his attention to me, prompting my deliberately wide eyes to look right past him, which seemed a convincing expression to adopt at the time.

'Mrs Thompson, we're going to need to call this in – do you understand? A senior officer will need to come out to the house, and they will arrange for crime scene investigators to inspect things, and for a coroner to remove the–' He wavered on his phrasing. 'Your husband. Do you understand that?'

My mother nodded her confirmation, prompting the officer to continue.

'Both yourself and your daughter will need to come down to the police station. You'll both need to answer some questions and make a statement. Do you understand that as well, Mrs Thompson?'

In response my mother spat out a blunt and confused 'No.'

A short silence followed this. One officer delivered a troubled look to the other.

'What is that you don't understand, Mrs Thompson?'

'Why we have to go, why you need us both. Why not just me?'

'It's procedure, Mrs Thompson, we have to do this.'

'Yes, but why?'

'Because someone has died,' he explained, as if maybe she hadn't realised.

Chapter three

There was nothing particularly interesting or enlightening about the investigation or the inquest that followed. I thought it might be useful, that I might learn something beyond what textbooks had offered me. In reality it was a tense handful of weeks to acquittal; the first third of my summer was spent with my mother and I both watching each other, waiting for signs that the other was about to crack. From years of dipping in and out of journals I had developed a rough timeline for how my hypothetical trial would go, and, fortunately, my mother's own trial followed a similar format. An array of unfamiliar neighbours elbowed their way into the proceedings (they would eventually invade our home as well, brandishing deepest sympathies and unappetising meals), and were paraded through the courtroom, holding up their polished opinions like honourable medals. They fought both for and against us, almost alternately, until time was called on the proceedings. The prosecution ran out of words long before my mother's defence did. We were, after all, two women who had lived in a violent household.

When the proceedings were finalised my mother didn't talk for four days. She had driven home in silence while I had made repeated phone calls regarding 'basic funeral packages'. However, after learning the outrageous costs associated with the whole thing, I gave some serious thought to the idea of boxing him up and burying him in the garden myself. The cardboard options offered by the likes of Compare the Casket were tempting, but I was unsure of the dimensions required for such a hole. Nor did I think I would be able to convince my mother that this was a fine idea.

'We'll pay whatever it takes to get rid of him,' she said. That was her only input.

For two days after that their bedroom became her tomb. At meal times she would peer out of the door, casting a cautious glance along the hallway before taking a step into it. I felt perturbed; surely the only person she was at risk of running into was me. Before venturing into the kitchen – at meal times that she had silently set and I had reluctantly adhered to – she allowed herself five minutes in the hallway, scrubbing at stains on the floor that only she could see.

Macbeth. 1599/1603/1606 (I can never quite decide). Lady Macbeth. 'Out, damned spot! Out, I say!'

And then my mother would retreat to her bedroom, clutching a meal that had grown cold during her cleaning.

'I can heat that up again for you.'

'You could eat that down here with me.'

'We can even eat in silence, if that's what you'd like.'

I had never been so accommodating before.

Alongside cooking, and a host of other household duties, the funeral arrangements made their way onto my to-do list. My mother didn't handle these early stages of grief particularly well, which a number of strangers assured me was quite normal. There were many days when my main source of conversation was provided by Bethany from Co-Operative Funeral Care. The house was silent and unloved, particularly by comparison to the ritualistic cleaning that took place prior to all of this. However, when the day of the funeral arrived, my mother lapsed into a state of complete uselessness that left me mourning her silence. Although I did try to be sympathetic towards her plight.

I shouted a thirty-minute warning ahead of leaving in the hope that this would be ample time for her to navigate her way into the dress I had ironed and hung out for her. It wasn't. When I went upstairs I found her perched on the edge of her unmade bed clutching the cup of tea I had taken up forty-eight minutes earlier. The dry toast – to settle her stomach – sat on the bedside table, untouched. An old shirt of my father's fell loosely off her shoulders, as if she had made an effort to remove the garment but had admitted defeat two buttons in. There were stains scattered over the fabric and I wondered which one of them this mess belonged to.

I checked my watch. We needed to leave in ten minutes.

In silence I dressed her. I rolled one leg of her nude-coloured tights up to her knee, before bunching up the other leg and repeating the process. I tugged the fabric up her thighs as far as I could before nudging her, to indicate that now was the time to move. I stretched the fabric a comfortable amount to lift it entirely over her buttocks before pulling my fingers around the elasticised edges and snapping the waistband against her skin.

'Mum, you need to lift your arms above your head now.'

She followed the instruction unashamedly, while I held a breath of panic inside my mouth; this was the closest I had been to a bare person before. With her arms raised in the air, I lifted the shirt over her head – avoiding the intimacy of buttons – and quickly replaced the shirt with the dress. One arm at a time, I fed the fabric over her until the loose-fitting garment hung about her on the bed.

'When you stand up this will fall better, I think.'

'I'm not ready, though.'

I must have missed something. Something obvious and crucial that another girl could never possibly have missed.

'I can't do this, love.'

'I don't think you're allowed to miss it. Or are you? I don't…'

'Gillian, what if I tell someone?'

'What if you tell someone what?'

'What if I tell someone what really happened?'

It was the first time that night had been mentioned since the inquest.

'What really happened, Mum?'

She shook her head and angled her face away from me. I knew she wouldn't answer.

'Have you told someone, Mum?' I asked, trying a different tactic.

'No, but I'm asking what if. What if it just slips out?'

Then I would have to kill them too.

She used the mirror as a means of watching me, scared of staring me directly in the eye.

'You'll just have to make sure it doesn't, won't you?'

I smiled at her through the mirror and although she matched this with a smile in return, it was obvious that she didn't mean it.

Throughout the day I kept my eyes on and around her; she had developed the look of an erratic woman on the verge of some sort of breakdown, which in many ways was appropriate for the occasion, but it still unsettled me. Her eyes refused to sit still, even when she was in mid-conversation, and her mouth straddled the line between a smile and a grimace for much of the event. By the time the funeral itself was concluded, her cheeks were so reddened and her hair sprang out with such enthusiasm that I wondered why I had gone to such lengths to make her look presentable before leaving the house.

At the wake – a party to celebrate the fact that the deceased was now six feet below ground level and was perhaps the only part of the day's events that I could lend my support to – the room was packed full of people who I had never seen before in my life. I assumed that they were customers, drinking associates, neighbours who had recently developed an inappropriate interest in my family. They took it in turns to approach my mother and me, as if perhaps they had drawn up a rota beforehand. After the first chorus of 'We were so sorry to hear the news' and 'If you need anything, you know where we are' the condolences became generic and the faces became a blur. In amongst all of this I lost my mother and became plagued by relentless imaginings of her confessing our shared sin to whoever would listen.

I tried to raise my line of vision over a mass of gravity-defying hair.

'Are you okay, my love?'

It was the favourite question of the day; the hot topic.

'I'm fine, thank you, I just need to find my–'

'How did you get on with that casserole?'

It transpired then that this woman – this stranger – had been one of many women to deposit food on our doorstep. Despite having no memory of having eaten her casserole specifically, I told her that the food had been well-received. She introduced herself as Anne Westburn from Number 34, and introduced the man-child, the overgrown Augustus Gloop slumped behind her, as her son, Timothy. The boy looked as unenthusiastic about attending my father's funeral as I was.

'I just want you to know that we are absolutely here for you, whatever you need, and your mother. Where is your mother? I've hardly had a glimpse of her what with this, well, this bustle of strangers,' Anne said, applying a tone of distaste to her final words. When she stepped back to scan the room my mother appeared across the room again, damp-eyed and in mid-conversation with a gentleman who looked horrified by whatever she had just said.

'I'll go and say a quick hello to her.' Number 34 disappeared and joined the queue that was forming around the room.

Little did I know that there was a queue forming around me too. Drama-hungry women in their mid-forties onwards flocked to me while their husbands maintained a safe distance, unsure of how to approach the emotionally fragile twenty-something girl that they perceived me to be. Twenty-eight minutes later, when this attention had settled, I found my mother again, enthusiastically sobbing on the shoulder of Number 34.

'He was my husband, for God's sake, it should have never, never have turned out this way. This just wasn't – it wasn't ever my plan.' Her speech was staggered around sobs that showed no signs of dissipating. The words were mostly inaudible as they soon intertwined with shoulder-shuddering sobs, while my mother's face became an image of the crying theatre mask. And the whole room, while trying to shoot sly glances in the direction of the grieving widow, willed her to continue.

Initially I had thought a small breakdown would be harmless, that it may have even added some authenticity to the event. However, as my mother's exclamations continued, I soon realised that she was treading dangerously close to a confession.

'He wasn't happy. God knows I wasn't happy, but this – this, I mean… how could this make anyone happy?' She spoke with the slurred incoherence of a drunk and I wondered whether perhaps she was.

'Sssh, pet, you did what you had to do.' Number 34 comforted her, blissfully ignorant.

Before she could deliver a slice of lukewarm comfort, my mother unleashed another wave of emotion, wailing with a ferocity that I had previously only heard emerge from animals. I admit now that I had underestimated the abusive bond shared between my parents during their marriage; I had no idea that their heartstrings had been so intertwined that this sudden pull would cause such an uncomfortable snap.

'I've been with him all my life. All my life, I haven't known anything different.'

I fought my way through the crowd and lowered myself down to her level; there was a flicker of something in her expression – fear, discomfort. Whatever it was, I didn't like it.

'I'm sorry, Gillian, I'm so sorry. I thought that I could, but I just can't.'

The possibilities for her apology were endless but I nevertheless felt the need to stifle it.

'Mum, you don't have anything to apologise for. You've done so well today.'

Accompanied by occasional cooing and shushing that went some way towards steadying her sobs, I removed my mother's tangled limbs from around Number 34 and placed her arms around my neck instead, steadily lifting her away from her seat as I stood. She moved with caution; a chimp changing handlers.

'Gillian, is there anything that I can–'

I cut Number 34 off before she could finish. 'Could you just explain to people? We're grateful to them for coming and providing their support, but it's been a taxing day and we thought it was perhaps best for us to slip away quietly.'

Star Trek. 1968. Leonard Nimoy. 'Oh, yes, you humans have that emotional need to express gratitude.'

I quickly added: 'Make sure you express our gratitude, won't you?'

As we tumbled out of the door of the building, my mother mumbled into my neck: 'Where are we going now then?'

'We're going home.'

'Why?'

A strand of saliva chased the question out of her mouth as her head dropped back against the passenger seat's headrest. For the majority of the journey that followed she remained slumped with her head against the window, a smudge of make-up following her along the glass whenever she shifted. Her breathing was heavy, relaxed; for the final ten minutes of the journey I couldn't decide whether she was even conscious. Then the wrench of the handbrake stirred her.

'We're home,' she announced, as if perhaps I hadn't noticed.

'Do you think you might be drunk?'

The only experience I'd had of drunken behaviour was that exhibited by my father, which seemed an inappropriate schema on which to base future incidents.

'I'm just so tired, Gillian.'

Despite her alleged exhaustion, she wouldn't let me help with her preparations for bed. Outside the door I waited until I could hear movement: a zip being pulled down; a drawer being opened. Downstairs, waiting for bread to toast and milk to warm, I put three relatively low dosage Diazepam tablets on a spoon before placing another spoon over the top and crushing them into a powder, which I stirred into the mug of warm milk.

Inside her bedroom I found her hunched over a wedding photograph that I had never seen. Tears dragged mascara from her eyes, down her cheeks, and on to the glass that protected their happy moment.

'I made you something to settle your stomach.'

It perhaps wasn't the right thing to say, but it was better than any alternatives I could construct at such short notice.

'Gillian, what are we going to do?'

'Right now I think you should eat something, and sleep.'

'That's not what I meant, love.'

'No, I didn't think that it was.'

She looked away from the frame and settled her eyes on the tray. I lifted the plate of toast and placed it on her night table, and then placed the mug of milk beside it, deliberately closer to her.

'You should drink that while it's warm. I don't think it helps as much when it gets cold.'

And, as instructed, she drank the whole thing in five thirsty mouthfuls.

The too-large duvet bunched up around her, leaving her small and childlike beneath it. I strategically borrowed one of her favourite moves from my childhood and, after tucking the quilt in around her, I leaned forward and left a single kiss on her forehead. It felt strange for the both of us, I suspect. I turned off the light, pulled the door shut, and waited downstairs for a little over an hour.

When I was confident she was asleep, I left the house and walked to my usual spot.

Chapter four

It was raining enough to be slightly cinematic. The moon was a convenient spotlight for him as he wandered towards me. This place had always been a popular area for his type. The worn wood of the park bench beneath me was growing more uncomfortable by the second but I couldn't move now; I knew that I'd grabbed his curiosity.

There was a jingle, like change in your pocket, as he clambered into the space next to me. I didn't make the first move despite being prepared to. Socio-cultural norms reminded me that as the woman I should wait for the male to make the initial contact. In my peripheral vision I could see that his eyes had settled on me. I counted down, setting deadlines only to immediately move them just before they were reached.

If he hasn't done something by X time…

I felt the outline of a skull nudge its way beneath my hand. His head was neatly cupped inside my left palm, as if the two were made for each other. As a result of his determined nuzzling, my fingertips collided with a bright red band wrapped around his neck; faux leather and sporting a small disc, the size and shape of a two-pound coin, it rattled beneath his padded chin. He was clearly well-fed, something that the majority of animal owners believe is synonymous with much-loved.

One side of the disc read: *If found please call…*

The other side had been branded with a name: Maurice.

'You don't look like a Maurice.'

He pulled away from me, lolling his head to one side in contempt or confusion, perhaps both. At this distance it became clear that behind the overgrown mop of black fur there were two brown button-like eyes, each iris sporting a collection of light-coloured flecks. As the rain persisted his fur became damp, ruffled, creating a severe edge to his appearance.

'I'm Gillian.'

His head rolled from one side to the other, his eyes narrowed.

'You don't look like a Gillian.' I could almost hear.

After this he reassumed his position, his head beneath my hand while the rest of him made efforts to creep closer towards me. I pressed my palm a little heavier against his brow while my fingers closed in tight enough to deliver something more than a squeeze. There came a low and satisfied rumble from somewhere inside his throat as I slowly released the pressure. I wasn't sure how much, if at all, he had enjoyed the crush, but it certainly went in my favour that he didn't stand up and leave.

'I imagine that you feel quite lucky, Maurice. Of all the crazy people you could have stumbled across this evening. Do you know, a week ago I read a story in a newspaper about a cat being set on fire while it was still alive, somewhere quite near here actually. It's disgraceful what some people will do to an animal.'

Eventually a self-stroking service was established. While my hand remained still on the roof of Maurice's head, he intermittently shifted himself about beneath it, simulating the sensation of being petted. The rumbles emerged from his throat at six-second intervals while his eyes half closed, forming a satisfied slant. For a second or two I envied what he must be feeling.

'What's it like, Maurice, to be so easily pleased?'

He threw his head backwards to regain control of my hand. He moved his body along the bench then, closing the small distance between us until my arm had encased him and his small ribcage was pressed neatly against my own. I held my breath and waited to feel the intake and expulsion of his. They breathe differently, you see. At the higher end of our average breathing beats per minute we are just about level with the slowest breathing rates of lesser animals – cats, for example. I took short and necessary breaths every few seconds, trying to intertwine them with Maurice's own.

I felt him living, quietly, for one minute and twenty-three seconds.

'I wonder how you ended up here, Maurice, with me. I wonder what it means that you did; if it means anything at all.'

I was disturbed by his vocal outburst, followed by my own: 'I can't let you go now.'

He tensed; I could feel his muscles shifting inside him. With an unexpected burst of energy he began to wriggle, pulling away from me as if his life depended on it. I pinned his abdominal area against my side with one hand holding his front legs steady; my other hand craned towards his neck. He persisted in throwing his head from one side to the other. My fingers fought through an excessive amount of damp fur before settling a grip around his throat.

A small, surprised wheeze escaped from his open mouth as pressure fell on his windpipe.

I really wanted it now, and this was taking too long.

I needed to see him, properly, before I could do anything else. I left one hand secured around his neck as I tucked the other beneath his stomach, keeping them both steady in their respective positions as I held him out in front of me. Suspended in mid-air, his hind legs thrashed about faster than I'd thought they'd be capable of given his size; his claws took repeated swipes at my forearms, enough for him to draw blood but not enough to be a deterrent. The park was abandoned at this time of night; it always had been. The streetlights that ran around the outer edge of the entrance didn't do much to light the inside space. I knew that Maurice and I were safe here. But I couldn't chase away the image, inappropriate though it was, of someone wandering in and observing this perverse reimagining of *The Lion King*.

I took a final proud look into his eyes before I jerked his head backwards. And it stayed there. His head sat at an abnormal position against the top of his spine while the unsettling crack seemed to swell in the space around us. He reminded me of a well-worn doll missing a chunk of stuffing as I lowered the body down.

The head hung off my leg with the consistency of excess fabric while the rest of him remained seated on my lap; the only sign of life now being the occasional ruffle of fur, prompted by the wind.

I picked through his coat, tracing the odd streaks of white and grey fur with my fingertips. Inhaling – one, two, three – and exhaling, I tried to keep hold of him for a second or two longer.

'I should say sorry.'

I held the body up to my face, rolled my nose through his smell, ran his fur along my lips, and listened for any last slips of life spilling out. As I stood up I continued to cradle him, supporting his head as you would with a newborn child. He looked as peaceful as I felt. I held him for a moment longer as the last of the tension slipped away from me. There was a lightness in my stomach that hadn't been there before, and I think I remember kissing him then. The same small and awkward kiss that I had, only three hours ago, left on my mother's forehead. And then I set him down on the bench; he lay on his side, legs outstretched, relaxing after a long evening stroll.

'I really should say sorry.'

I could barely convince myself to move. I wondered who would find him, what they would do with him; would he be okay? He was too big to fit alongside the other specimens, and I would struggle to find a jar to hold his frame. But, despite knowing this, it still didn't feel right to leave him behind. I pinched his front right paw between my finger and thumb, feeling his rough pads, weathered from years of wandering. I could have brought something with me – a scalpel, a small box – to take a piece of him away, but the opportunity had passed now. I had no choice but to leave him.

Crouching level with the seat, I leaned forward and planted another small kiss on his head. Then I walked away, wondering, again, who might find him.

Chapter five

You want to know what it's like. I can understand that; I wanted to know as well, I suppose. Ultimately, it's like anything else that any one person does despite knowing that they shouldn't. But they do it all the same, because they're too familiar with the feeling that they'll experience afterwards.

Life is so heavy most of the time. You're struggling under the surface with a weight on you and what do you do? How do you find a way to breathe again? We're all dying to know the answer – and don't think that I haven't noticed the wonderful irony there – but, lacking any feasible explanations for life's largest dilemmas and questions, instead we simply guess. We assume things that will improve our little existence. And these assumptions, they then become our unashamed justifications for whatever condemnable behaviours we throw ourselves into. 'It makes life a little better,' we say, excusing our tendencies to cheat on our partners, overeat unhealthy foods, smoke. It makes life a little better, and for the majority of us that is reason enough for anything.

Does any of this sound familiar? There must be something – one mostly harmless little thing – that you allow yourself. That one cigarette at the end of the day; that eye contact with a colleague you hold for a beat too long?

'No human beings were harmed in the making of this bad habit,' we remind ourselves; a disclaimer to our misdemeanours. It's only a problem, you see, when people become aware of it, when people are hurt by it. That's when the masses will frown and judge – as though that has become the benchmark for human depravity. You've hurt another human being? Well, that's a line! But it's a line that we love to see crossed, don't you think? There's nothing better than finding someone more evil than ourselves because those people really put things into perspective.

'I might be doing *this* but at least I'm not doing *that*. Besides, who is it even hurting?' Oh, wait, you know who I'm really hurting now, don't you?

Playing the poor girl from the damaged home is difficult, especially now you know this much of the story. Maybe the reality is closer to the poor home from the damaged girl; maybe we'll never know which came first. There are – or at least there would be, if I discussed these issues openly and honestly with a medical practitioner – theories. In fact science could likely offer several feasible interpretations of and explanations for this situation. Sociopathy, psychopathy, narcissistic personality disorder (that last one seems unavoidable, really). Someone would find a textbook explanation of a power-hungry only child whose inherent egotism interacted poorly with overexposure to violence during her attachment-forming years. The abuse – my father's penchant for abuse – would play a part in their discussion. It may even be the hook of their discussion; I understand that abuse is often the first thing that they look for in these circumstances. They would find it and use it to great effect, I'm sure, because it's neat. It's a tidy explanation for every damaged and/or defective element of my personality and they have to offer little to no insight into me as an autonomous individual then. What a bonus. They can explain it away with nature versus nurture discussions around the family home and parental values, and society can take something of a back seat. Although it will inevitably play its part as well, because doesn't it always these days?

We like to explain away the deranged logic of killing things as quickly and efficiently as we can. The people who do it, well, they're a biological anomaly; look at who they grew up with – *with a name like that I'd murder people too*! Even though killing is one of the most human things about us, really. It's what we're built for. People will need to believe that I kill things because of biology/society/daddy issues, or a horrendous combination of the three. It would be the last thought to cross the general population's mind – assuming it has a functioning one these days – that I do it because I want to, or because I need to. And it is a need, I think – deep-rooted, inherent, human. We lost our way somewhere along the evolutionary chain but this behaviour is normal. There was a time when all humans did was gut animals and rut; we're too politically correct for the former now, and far too liberal with the latter.

For my own curiosity then, tell me: what shocked you more, the animal with the broken neck or the patricide? Really take some time to consider that, and then tell me why I'm the only monster here.

Morally, you're right to believe that it's wrong. There's not a textbook or an essay in the world that would correct you – at least, not one that I can find. So yes, it is wrong – but it's also required. It's a compulsive cure as much as cheating, overeating, smoking.

Q. Why does he cheat?
A. Because it feels good.

Q. Why does she smoke?
A. Because it calms her down.

Q. Why do I kill things?
A.

Well, picture this: it's been a long day. You come home and eat an inadvisable amount of something that will offend your arteries. You watch the news, which further compounds your ambiguous mood, and you make dinner. When walking from the kitchen to the dining room with your dinner, you spill a significant measurement of your accompanying beverage on the floor – and you cry. In the grand scheme of things – with a news report delivering word of another random stabbing in the background – this is an inconsequential incident and your emotional outpouring is disproportionate to the tragedy of a spilled drink. But, my

God, you cry. Like someone greeted with the threat of perpetual torment, until your eyelashes are sodden and your lungs have a debilitating stutter. Then you continue to cry, like the world is about to come to an end and for a moment, in between the third and fourth moment of crying, you quietly hope that it will. And when you run out of tears, your face is sore and your eyes are swollen, and your lips are resuming their usual lineation rather than the misshapen downturn they've held for the minutes prior to this, you are a visual mess; but you feel a hell of a lot better than you did half an hour ago.

Q. Why do I kill things?
A. See above.

That's the closest I can get to explaining it. It might not be close enough, I know. There's a decent chance that you will read that and still not understand, assuming that you even want to understand such behaviour. You might even still be curious about why, how, what it's like. The kill is the cry and the afterburn is the deepest exhale, a shoulder-sagging sigh that leaves you empty, ready to be filled again by the world and your day-to-day struggles in it. There's nothing quite as refreshing as breaking up life with your hands. But even after all of this, I'm still not sure that I'd recommend it.

You're probably safer with smoking.

Chapter six

My mother had never been the questioning kind; perhaps that was due to years spent living with my untameable father. Perhaps that's also why, in his absence, she suddenly felt moved to ask all of the questions that her mind could muster. Where are you going? Who with? How long do you think you'll be?

'You're going out again?'

My right hand was just a centimetre above the lock on the front door when my mother lassoed me. It was a difficult question to answer. I thought from my attire and from my angle towards the exit it was clear that yes, I was going out again, but it was also clear to me that that was not the answer that my mother was expecting.

'I thought you were sleeping,' I replied, instantly aware that this wasn't the right response either.

My mother had taken to napping in the afternoons. The days of frantic cleaning from morning until late in the day had been stuffed inside my father's coffin alongside him, and my mother now spent her days pining. Maintaining her role of downtrodden housewife, she would quietly sweep up, tidy away what she referred to as clutter, and when those menial tasks were dealt with, she would indulge in some quiet time. She read, occasionally, and stared at the damned spot in the hallway frequently, like she expected something about it to change. And then, at around this time every day, she slept, exhausted from her morning of mourning.

'Why are you going out all the time now?' she asked, with a greater measure of suspicion than I thought the question warranted.

'That's what normal people do, Mum.'

I had no idea whether that was true or not but it seemed a feasible argument, and when my mother nodded and disappeared back into the living room I assumed that it must have been an acceptable one too. She was right, of course; I was going out more. Chiefly to escape my mother who these days needed more interactions than I was capable of providing, but also to see these so-called normal people – the ones who I thought might be out there. I had tried libraries, coffee shops, parks – although the latter was too closely associated with my less-normal activities – and on that evening my destination of choice was a restaurant.

It turned out to be one of those cliché places, solely lit by candles and occupied by couples. The walls were decorated with chalkboards, cheap artistic prints, and odd-angled shelves that displayed empty wine bottles. There were six couples already in the room by the time I arrived, all seated a safe distance from each other.

'Table for one, lady?'

Without waiting for confirmation the short, plump man grabbed a menu and marched away from the couples, leading me to a table for two tucked away in a corner. A large part of me was tempted to turn for the exit, but it wasn't often that I was given the opportunity to observe this style of interaction in real life. Much of my romance schema had been fed by romantic comedies, and I was aware of their likely artifice. And so I followed him.

The man deposited my menu on the table and nodded towards one of the chairs.

'You sit here, lady, we take order soon.'

I wondered whether the Italian accent and poor English were authentic. Before I had time to make a decision, another interruption arrived – a new voice, speaking in loud and unaccented English:

'Of all the corners, in all the restaurants, in all the towns, she walks into mine.' *Casablanca*. 1942. Humphrey Bogart. But it wasn't quite right.

In my initial scan of the room I had missed someone. Two tables away from where I was sitting, there sat another solitary diner at a table for two, in the lonely corner of the restaurant.

'I'm not sure you've got the quote right,' I replied, raising my voice to travel across the furniture partition between us.

'I'm sure I haven't,' he admitted, not seeming to mind. 'I just needed an opener.'

He smiled and so I smiled in return, feeling I should. He was a conventionally attractive young man of average build and height, from what I could gather, although his sitting position made it challenging to properly judge. But he was pleasing enough to the eye, with a neat albeit lopsided smile and hair tucked up into something that nearly resembled a quiff. He didn't wear glasses, although he appraised the room with a squint that suggested he needed them. His clothing created the illusion of someone slightly older, but his face belonged to someone in the same age bracket as myself.

'Sometimes the movies can say things better than I can.' He shrugged.

My smile that followed this was much more authentic than my first. There was something all too familiar in his sentiment.

On the table in front of him there sat a half-empty bottle of Corona. There was one menu and one place setting, also directly in front of him, and one set of cutlery. There was no coat draped over the back of the chair opposite, nor a handbag hidden beneath it. When I looked back to the young man I saw that while I had surveyed his surroundings, he had surveyed me. He smiled before speaking again.

'Do you mind if I scooch over a little towards you? There's a fair bit of distance with all

these tables here in the way.'

My cheeks began to burn with what felt like frustration – although I couldn't say whether it was directed at the young man or at myself. I had walked into this situation.

He tucked a well-worn corduroy blazer beneath his arm before picking up his menu and his bottle and migrating over to the empty seat opposite me. A grating sound caused me to wince as he pulled his chair closer to the table, dragging the legs along the floor. When he felt close enough to the table to be comfortable, he took a second to smooth down the front of his shirt – it was a strange off-white with a brown stripe, presumably picked to match his brown blazer. He appeared to think he had just sat down to a job interview rather than to dinner with a stranger. I wondered whether his schemas were the same for both.

As he settled himself into the chair, it occurred to me that I had probably missed my opportunity to halt his plans. Or had I? I could have still stopped him, I suppose. But when would an incident like this occur again? A one-to-one conversation with a stranger for a prolonged period of time would be a challenge, but it may also be a worthwhile undertaking.

'I'm Daniel.'

'Gillian.'

'That's a pretty name, Gillian.'

'Thank you, Daniel. Yours is…' I stumbled over the compliment. 'Also nice.'

Following the formula for a conventional introduction, Daniel promptly stuck his arm out across the table; at the end of his arm there was a flat and expectant palm. I took a quick glance at his face to search for signs of humour or irony. Blue eyes looked back at me; the shade was so bright that you seldom find it in adults. His mouth was pulled up at one side in a lazy-looking smile that caused an indent in his cheek.

'Sometimes, when people are meeting for the first time, they shake hands.'

'I'm not sure it's singularly associated with the first meeting.'

'Ah, so you are familiar with the gesture.'

I took his hand and delivered an abrupt shake; his palm was sweaty.

'You have a good handshake, Gillian.'

'I didn't realise you could classify handshakes.'

'Absolutely! There's too firm, where you fear for the safety of your fingers; too limp, where your hand comes away feeling a little insulted. And there are unfathomable types in between those. Yours is certainly one of the better ones.' He pressed his palm against his chest before he continued: 'And I really do mean that.'

The whole situation felt highly irregular, increasingly so, as the minutes rolled by.

Fargo. 2014. Billy Bob Thornton. 'No, highly irregular is the time I found a human foot in a toaster oven. This is just odd.'

Trying to regain some perspective, I asked: 'Daniel, do you often eat dinner with strangers?'

I was certain this behaviour wasn't actually normal practice, but Daniel had taken to it with such ease that I had to check. He relaxed against the back of his chair, as if the question would take some serious thought, then said: 'Well, it's better than eating alone, isn't it?'

We perused our menus after that, with Daniel occasionally interrupting the quiet:

'Do you think you'll have a starter?'

'Are you more of a pudding person?'

'How do you feel about salmon?'

'And what about people who eat salmon?'

'Should I have some sort of grievance with people who eat salmon?' I asked.

'It's hard to say. I'm sure you could if you tried; you seem the type.'

We ordered a bottle of red wine and two steaks. Daniel wanted his well done, I wanted mine as close to rare as they were comfortable serving it.

'How can you eat your steak like that?' Daniel quizzed.

'It's better when it's bloody.'

'Well, there's a life motto that I can live without.' He laughed, but I was unsure why his remark had been amusing to him. Part of me – the desperate-to-conform part – wanted to laugh with him; the observational part just wanted to know what this Daniel character might do next. 'So, Gillian,' he started again. 'What is the wildest thing you've ever done in your entire life?'

The steaks were set on the table just as Daniel completed his question. He tucked in immediately, pouring himself half a glass of wine before grabbing at his cutlery. He clearly expected me to hold the conversation. It was tempting to squash the naiveté of his question with a truly honest answer and, although I barely knew the boy in front of me, I believed that my not knowing him was part of his appeal. I could have been entirely honest with him, and then just walked away. Would we walk away, though? Was that actually how this would end? In the thirteen seconds it took me to consider this, Daniel began to speak again, apparently noting the unexpected difficulty of his question.

'That was probably a little unfair, actually. Shall I go first?'

I nodded.

'Okay, when I was seven, maybe eight – although, I don't suppose my age has much to do with the story, so we'll just say seven slash eight – I took a book out of the library using my mum's library card, and, well, to this day I still haven't taken it back.' At that he theatrically dropped his cutlery onto his plate and leaned back in his chair, releasing a deep sigh as he did so. 'You have no idea how good it feels to finally get that off my chest.'

Despite my best efforts to remain unmoved, I smiled.

'Is that true?'

'Are you silently judging me for being a juvenile thief?'

'No, I'm judging you for being so boring.'

'Interesting. So you're not opposed to theft, then? Now, is that generally or is it specifically a book thing?'

'What book was it?'

'Do you know something, Gillian, of all the people in the world to hear that sordid tale, you are the first person to ask that question.'

'I'm wondering whether it was worth stealing.'

'*The Strange Case of Dr Jekyll and Mr Hyde.*'

It seemed a peculiar book for anyone to steal, but it said a lot about him.

As the evening progressed I found that I was beginning to like Daniel. Over the course of four and three-quarter hours, two steaks, several more glasses of wine – Daniel was more of a drinker than me – and one and a half desserts, we established that Daniel had recently moved to this area, to care for an aunt who was now battling cancer. It was just Daniel – he had no siblings – and his two healthy but self-centred parents had relocated to Nice to live the great cliché – Daniel's words – leaving him responsible for the remainder of their affairs in the United Kingdom. Prior to the business with his aunt, Daniel's profession had officially been 'financial assistant', which he assured me was as boring as it sounded. He believed comedies to be the superior genre of film; he liked music mostly taken from the charts, but he preferred to tell women that he listened to jazz because he believed that it added something charming to his persona; and when he didn't sleep through his weekend alarm, he always made the effort to attend church on a Sunday.

'I'm just saying, if God wanted us all to get up at the crack of dawn every Sunday morning then he wouldn't have gone and called it the day of rest. Am I right, or am I right?'

I couldn't decide whether the question was rhetorical.

Daniel was making eyes at the half-eaten chunk of brownie on the plate in front of me when he spoke again. 'If I remember my law studies correctly, it's actually a little bit illegal to leave something that looks that good,' he said.

'You're welcome to finish it.'

'No judgement?'

I shook my head. He pulled the plate towards him and, turning the fork on its side to score a line along the brownie, he then pulled away a decent-sized chunk which he slipped into his mouth. He let out a series of exaggerated 'Mmms' and 'Ahhs' as he chewed his way through the generously sized piece. When he had finished his performance he set his fork down and grabbed a napkin. He dabbed at the corners of his mouth, catching one or two stray flecks of chocolate.

'Now you know everything about me, including my dark history of fraudulent behaviour, and my penchant for anything made of chocolate, and I don't even know so much as your favourite colour.'

'Yellow.'

He grimaced.

'What's wrong with yellow?' I asked.

'Isn't it something to do with death? You always see it, don't you, on funeral cars and headstones and, well, just where death is I suppose.' He drained the remains of his wine glass and glanced at his watch. 'Christ, I think I have stolen far too much of your time, and my own, come to think of it. So, Gillian of Yellow, I shall pack up, pay up, and go home with little to no knowledge of the woman with whom I have just spent an entire evening.' He wiped away a faux tear.

As I turned to search for my purse in my coat pocket he continued: 'Please?' He gestured with his wallet as he spoke, as if it were a part of the question. 'I'm sure you weren't too fussed about having my company and you were just too polite to tell me; the least I can do is pay for your dinner.'

Not for the first time that evening, I felt unsure of what was happening. But then I felt equally unsure of how, or even if, I could decline Daniel's offer. The evening had, after all, adopted the conventional structure of a date – much as the term and indeed the conduct perturbed me. Also, as modern society would have you believe, the male, whether by pride or as a throwback to hunter-gatherer ancestry, is somehow inherently inclined to pay for the pleasure of feeding his female companion. I smiled and nodded then.

'It has been–' I paused and wondered how to complete the sentence.

'Irritating? Demanding? Blood-boiling?'

'Pleasant. I think it's been pleasant.'

Daniel clenched his fist in mock anguish. 'Damn it! Pleasant would have been my next guess. Although, I suppose there's nothing wrong with pleasant, is there, Gillian of Yellow?'

'Thompson.'

'Oh, at last, Gillian Thompson tells me something. And now, if you're feeling generous, tell me something else, Miss Thompson: What is the wildest thing you've ever done in your life?'

'At the beginning of the summer, I killed someone.' I remained neutral as I spoke, as if this were the most natural answer in the world for someone to give to such a question.

'Pretty wild, Gillian Thompson.' He paused deliberately, as if considering how he could move the conversation on from this. 'Doesn't really compare to the whole library book thief thing. Does it?'

Chapter seven

The outside world seemed brighter than it had a few hours ago. Not in a metaphorical sense. The sky was a light charcoal with intermittent smudges of clouds and the stars were spread out erratically, as if a child had gained control of a glitter shaker. And it was good to be alone. I hadn't realised how disruptive Daniel had been over the course of the evening but as I walked home I greatly appreciated the quiet that accompanied me.

I avoided the bench on the way. It made the journey longer but it felt necessary, although I struggled to decipher why. At three minutes past midnight I arrived outside my mostly dark house, though there was a glow emanating from the living room. It was clear that behind those closed curtains there was a low-watt bulb still wide awake, and although I listened carefully on my approach I couldn't hear a noise to go with it. No television; no late-night phone call to the Samaritans.

Reluctant to ruin the serenity of the moment, I placed my key into the front door with great care. I had a vision of my mother's head snapping towards the sound and so I slowed to complete the manoeuvre as quietly as I could. I pressed against the inside lock until I heard the second click. I pulled the larger lock across (for our safety, although the monsters had always lived inside the house), and I waited.

After a minute I took three steps forward, bringing me level with the living room door. My mother was sitting upright in my father's old armchair, her body angled towards the television screen that showed nothing but static. The combination of the lazy table lamp and the crackling glow from the television lit the room in an uncomfortable way. Her head allowed for a quick twitch to the side as my footsteps became more pronounced. After an evening laden with human interaction, it was tempting to back away and to leave my mother alone to contend with any breakdown that she might be having. But her expression concerned me. She was, after all, my mother.

'I think that's quite bad for your eyes, Mum.'

There came another head twitch. This one steadily evolved into a shake. I turned the television off and the room became notably darker, yet enough light remained for me to garner a good view of my mother's expression. The bags beneath her eyes had swollen into small cushions; the cheeks beneath them were overrun with red blotches competing for space. Train tracks of mascara had run down each cheek in a way that I recognised from the funeral.

'Have you been crying?'

'Yes.'

'Why?'

'Where have you been tonight?'

Conversational exchanges have never been my strong point, but even I could tell that there was something misshapen about this interaction.

'I went for a walk to begin with but then it rained–'

'Where did you walk?'

'Out to the public park, just outside–'

'Why did you go there?'

'Why do you keep interrupting me?'

It was the first time she had looked at me since I had entered the room. There was a hardness to her eyes that I didn't recognise. I wondered whether she'd been drinking but a quick scan of the room showed no empty bottles, cans, or glasses.

'You've been out all evening. That's a long time.'

'I wanted some air and so I started walking. I didn't think much about it until I stopped.'

'That sounds like a little lie, Gillian.'

I didn't know what response she was expecting. Stumped, I continued with my itinerary.

'It started raining while I was out so I found somewhere to have dinner as well, and now

I'm home. That's my whole evening.'

She narrowed her eyes as though she were physically inspecting the words. Her mouth was tucked up at one side in a sort of smirk, implying a level of self-assurance that seemed inappropriate for my mother's general character. I couldn't help but return to the idea that an alcoholic stimulant might be involved here. No, there was no evidence, but my mother had spent enough time clearing up after my father to know how to clear up after herself.

'Mum, have you been drinking?'

'Worse, love, I've been thinking.' A high-pitched squeak followed. It later occurred to me that it was a laugh.

'Do you want to tell me why you've been crying?'

Her mouth dropped, her head shook, and a small puff of air escaped from her. 'You can't work it out, love?'

'Dad?'

'What else could there possibly be to cry about?' Although it was a question, something

about her intonation suggested that she wasn't looking for an answer. 'I'm struggling here, Gillian.'

'Struggling with me?'

I thought that must have been the case. Otherwise, why tell me?

'Struggling with…' She paused and lifted her arms in a defeatist gesture. 'This.' She looked up, but I couldn't bring myself to look back. 'Love, are you struggling at all?'

That time I did look at her, involuntarily; a knee-jerk reaction response to her question. Biologically speaking there are occasions when certain elements of the human body react ahead of the rest of it. This was an embarrassing case of a physical reaction prefacing a vocal or mental one, and when I was looking her directly in the eye I knew that it was too late to retract the move. Continuing with the so-called natural response, my mouth fell open slightly in the prelude to speech. I hoped that an 'Of course' or an 'I can't believe you're asking that' would chase after the gesture, but my mother intervened before I had the chance to force the sentiment.

'I do worry for you, Gillian.'

'For me?'

'With all this. With all that happened.' She paused and puffed out her cheeks. Her head tilted slightly from one side to the other as if she were trying to gauge the physical weight of what she was about to say. 'Maybe we should talk about this in the morning, love.'

I said nothing about the fact that my mother had stayed awake to have this conversation. Whatever 'this' was, I agreed with her that yes, it would be better discussed after sleep. The unanswered query regarding my mother's alcohol intake was all too apparent when she attempted to lever herself from the seat beneath her, exhibiting the same struggle that my father had often experienced. From this angle, there was a disturbing similarity between the two of them. With one arm wrapped around her, and tucked neatly beneath her left armpit, I helped my mother up to bed. When she breathed a goodnight kiss against my cheek, the alcohol was unmistakable.

***

I had always hated the smell of bacon. Yet I had a distinct childhood memory of my mother cooking it the morning after my father's binges, or his incidents, although the terms seem somewhat interchangeable given that we seldom experienced one without the other. And so the following morning when an enthusiastic sun slipped through my curtains, I made my bed, got dressed, and shifted downstairs to make breakfast for my mother. While the meat hissed in the frying pan I stood next to the open window on the other side of the kitchen, pulling in mouthful after mouthful of fresh air. With the bacon held out at arm's length I turned it, begrudgingly, to evenly cook its surface before retreating to the safe side of the room where

I buttered bread. I was midway through the second round when the door let out a small creak and my mother appeared.

'You look dreadful.'

'Thank you, Gillian,' she said, rubbing her face as she spoke. 'But I feel surprisingly chipper, all things considered.'

She made no further comment on what all these considered things were and I didn't push the issue.

'I thought breakfast might help.'

'That's nice of you, love, but I really just need some tea.'

I was midway to the table, clutching a small plate on top of which sat a bacon sandwich, when she made this announcement. She looked from the sandwich to me and flashed a thin smile before leaning away from the table.

'Pop it down, maybe I'll manage it after some tea.' She looked the food over with more suspicion than seemed necessary. 'You hate bacon, love.'

I nodded confirmation and moved to the kettle, unsure of what to do with her remark.

'If you hate bacon, why did you cook it?'

'You used to cook bacon for Dad when he'd had a lot to drink.'

'Gillian, I...' She paused there, perhaps trying to collect together enough words to construct a coherent explanation for her behaviour. 'Sometimes you just need a drink, love.'

Animal House. 1978. John Vernon. 'Fat, drunk, and stupid is no way to go through life.' Not that my mother was fat.

I threw teabags into cups, added small measures of milk, and set the kettle to boil. As it did so, I turned to survey my mother and found her elbows balanced on the kitchen table, her head firmly planted in her hands. At some point the bacon sandwich had been pushed an additional ten inches away from her, which just seemed rude. I completed the task in silence and set a full mug of tea down in front of her.

'Maybe that will make you feel better,' I offered, although I had no memory of it ever having worked for my father. I quietly hoped it wouldn't work for her.

She held the mug close to her face and blew over the edge of it, twice, three times, before taking a measured sip. When the liquid hit her lips, she winced.

'Too hot?'

'Just a little, love, yes.'

Funny that, you blew on it and everything.

'Gillian, I want us to talk about what happened with your dad.'

I nodded but said nothing.

'Do you have anything you'd like to say, about what happened?'

There was something – it may have been a small flicker of panic – hovering in my lower abdomen when she completed her sentence. I simply puffed my cheeks, turned down the corners of my mouth, and shook my head. A 'Nope, nothing there' sort of gesture, I hoped. My mother closed her eyes and shook her head. She expelled a breath. Her hands released their grip on her mug of tea and she placed them, palms down, on the table.

'I'm going to stay with your aunt Jackie for a few days. Why don't you come with me?'

I hadn't seen Jackie since we had moved into this house some eleven years ago. She was particularly vocal about her disapproval of my parents' marriage. Because of that, my father had been particularly vocal about us having nothing more to do with her.

'I didn't realise that you were in touch with her.'

'I called her last night, before you came home.'

She paused, leaving a beat that I felt obliged to fill.

'How is she?'

'Concerned, mostly, love.'

'About you?'

My mother rolled her eyes, creating an expression that I suspected I wasn't meant to notice, before confirming that yes, Jackie was concerned about her. Between the two of us we managed to construct a coherent enough chat regarding Jackie and her current whereabouts – Cornwall, it turned out, had been her hideaway after the fall-out with Mum, and she now couldn't bring herself to leave the place. We even covered the brief details of what she had been doing with herself more generally over the last decade or so. I won't bore you with the specifics of that. The quick explanation is: not much.

'You're not talking about what happened with your dad, Gillian, and you're obviously not keen on talking about it either. And, well, it worries me, love. Jackie, she's always been good at the talking thing, you know, being the big sister and all.'

It felt like a tenuous link but with a flick of my hand and an enquiring expression, I encouraged her to continue.

'I think a few days away might help. We can talk, really talk, about what happened, and how you're feeling about it, and how we move forward from here. And I know you haven't seen Jackie in a long time, but she's a good talker, like I said, and she'd like to help us.' She paused, sighed, and then finished off with: 'What do you think?'

I remember thinking lots of things at that moment in time. But above all, I remember thinking that I should have expected this. I should have seen this sort of intervention perched on the horizon; I should have seen it hurtling towards me. Perhaps noting this hesitation, my mother pressed forward with yet another helpful comment:

'You need to talk about what happened, love, and if you can't talk to family then who can you talk to?'

The question, it transpired, was largely rhetorical. So, when I said, 'A healthcare professional?' my mother was, perhaps, quite within her rights to be so surprised.

'You'd prefer to see someone?'

Having a heart to heart with a stranger was a favourable alternative to having a heart to heart with my misshapen mother and her estranged sister, yes. Of course it was.

'I think so, yes,' I replied.

'But you realise there are only certain things you can say to a stranger.'

I stifled a smile. It had been some time since my mother had spoken to me like a child.

'Mum, what are you really worrying about here?'

The silence held up for just shy of eight seconds before she answered.

'You've been involved with a terrible accident, and you aren't saying anything about it.' Her careful phrasing had done nothing to dissuade me from seeing someone. Not if the only real alternative was to discuss it with her (and Jackie?) instead. I promised that I would see a professional. The pledge was so convincing that it was only a minute later that my mother was discussing her plans to visit Jackie again.

'It hardly seems fair to leave you on your own, love. It's not right, is it.'

It was a statement but she looked for an answer. I was familiar with the tactic so offered: 'I think it's a difficult time for both of us, Mum, and if you feel like you'd benefit from visiting Jackie for a few days, then I'll support your decision.' I smiled, and then added: 'Just like you're supporting my decision not to.'

My mother disappeared to pack a small suitcase. She was taking the train down to Cornwall so that she could leave the car – my car, I assumed, given she hadn't driven my father's at all since his death – with me, in case I needed it. I thanked her, despite not feeling altogether sure why I was doing so, and then offered to drive her to the train station. We remained comfortably quiet with each other until we arrived at the station's designated drop-off zone.

'You will see someone about this, love, soon?' she said, before she slid out of the passenger seat.

I nodded. 'Of course, Mum.'

'You really need to, Gillian.' She leaned back in and planted a small kiss on my cheek. 'And you will be okay for a couple of days?'

The question seemed redundant now given that she had already decided to leave.

'I'll be fine. I just want you to concentrate on looking after yourself for a change, Mum.' I couldn't recall which film I had borrowed the sentiment from, but I felt certain that it was one of the most sincere things I had ever said to her.

Chapter eight

There was something unsettling about the house after she'd left. I felt like I was trespassing behind enemy lines, waiting to be caught. An average twenty-two-year-old would probably have felt delighted by this freedom, but I was not average, and even the proposed period of time left me feeling anxious. How long was a few days, precisely? This concern, combined with a cavalcade of others – was she seeing Jackie? What had she told her? Would she even come back? – meant that it just slipped my mind to feel excited.

I filled the new silence by boiling the kettle, toasting bread, slicing cheese. The doorbell chimed in then as well.

'Morning, Gillian dear!'

The words hit my ears before the door was fully opened. Number 34's smile was too wide, too bright, but the slumped-up mass of teenage hormones that hovered behind her went some way towards counteracting it.

'I'm surprised to see you,' she said, in a tone that sounded authentic, although I couldn't fathom why – I did live there, after all. 'You remember my son?'

How could I forget?

'Of course,' I replied.

'Is your mother about, dear?'

She leaned in as she spoke, taking a peek about inside the doorway like she expected my mother to be loitering, just waiting for her arrival.

'Was she expecting you?'

It seemed a fair question but her expression became puzzled.

'Well, no, she wasn't. You're quite right. This is ever so rude of me.'

I was right: this was rude of her. But I was sure that I hadn't actually said that.

'It's nothing important – why I wanted to see her, I mean; it's just that I brought this over,' she said, handing me a fabric bag that was packed to bursting. 'I've made up some more food, you see, after you said how much you liked the casserole. It's just a few bits and pieces, different things that you can pop in the microwave. You have a microwave?'

What sort of household did she think this was?

'Yes, we have a microwave.'

She played at wiping her forehead before she spoke again.

'Phew. And your mother isn't around at all?'

'She has been struggling lately. I'm sure you can understand.'

She answered me with a thin-lipped smile and a 'Mm.'

'She's actually away visiting my aunt at the moment. She left this morning. I'll mention you when I speak to her, and pass on your concerns.'

Number 34 hovered, as if I hadn't quite provided enough information yet. An exhale of genuine relief flooded from me when the house phone started to ring somewhere in the background. With a faux apology from myself and an overtly polite 'Oh, of course, dear,' from Number 34, I was finally able to excuse myself from the situation.

It was my mother. My still-inquisitive mother, it seemed. We talked briefly about whether I was coping alone, whether I needed her to come home, whether I was okay, and, two minutes later, whether I was still okay. It had been a day, I reminded her, and I was managing just fine, even though I expressed the sentiment with underwhelming conviction. She had never asked so many questions and I had never felt so bitter about having to supply any one person with quite so many answers. I was relieved to say goodbye to her. The conversation was hardly deep, merely repetitive, but the emotion she forced down me had become clogged in my throat somehow during my attempts to digest it. I needed a change of scenery, a walk, and perhaps something else.

Years of making meticulous observations had allowed me to determine that the afternoon dog walk was typically the household responsibility of the woman. That afternoon there was a vast array of so-called designer dogs around Runner's Route, with their designer owners in tow, both constructed to be petite, pleasant to look at, but utterly insignificant. I wandered along the path as a woman in a purple velour tracksuit jogged ahead of me. Her tracksuit was a perfect match for the purple of her Labradoodle's collar, and I wondered how much money it had cost her husband to make that coincidence happen – whether he even knew that was what he was paying his wife for.

I walked further, trying to shake off the medley of feelings sitting in my stomach. I thought of my father, my mother, of Daniel – why Daniel? – as I walked, and, thankfully, after thirty-four minutes of observing the same woman on repeat, divine intervention struck. The dog – accompanied by its male owner – rounded the corner unexpectedly and caught my attention within seconds.

It was a spectacular-looking animal, and it far surpassed the standards set by those around it. Its legs were strong, with distinct thigh muscles that suggested remarkable physical ability, and it boasted a heavyset jaw that looked equipped to crush the animals that surrounded it. The dog's owner paused for breath in what had apparently been a furious run for them both, and that's when the teeth appeared. It broke into an exhausted pant, revealing a set of well-maintained fangs that belonged to a hunting animal.

They settled on a bench some nineteen feet away from my own and enjoyed a moment of rest. The man removed a small sports bottle from the support band around his waist and took three measured mouthfuls from the container. Without hesitation, he up-ended the bottle and held the dripping mouthpiece out towards the animal in front of him; it maintained its military stance but extended its neck towards the bottle, creating an audible slap each time its tongue caught the liquid. The surrounding women appeared to find the whole display endearing; they illustrated this with a string of stares and coos that became more pronounced. One woman even attempted to make contact; she laid a patronising pat on the animal's head before saying something to the owner and laughing. His face remained steady, unimpressed.

It really was remarkable. I had never seen something so well-built. It would never fit in the box; it had enough strength to fight back; it would be missed. And yet, it was undeniably attractive to me. The dog's tongue hung limp from the side of its mouth while it panted, gulping down air and pausing only to slap its top and bottom jaw together long enough to wet its mouth, before the jaw dropped open again. It fidgeted a little, while remaining seated, its leg muscles contracting from the intense exercise. Sweat dripped from his forehead and a hand rose up to wipe away the liquid, rub at the back of a damp neck, and then pat the equally exhausted dog.

I had no idea which one of them I had been watching.

They remained seated for five minutes and thirty-two seconds. As they both attempted to regulate their breathing I found myself wondering how long they had been running for – how often they ran. The animal remained seated, panting, its tongue hanging limply from the left side of its mouth, creating an altogether less intimidating expression than the one it had started with. It threw occasional glances in the direction of its owner before eventually clambering back to its feet, to indicate that now would be a good time to leave. The owner smiled in recognition, which said he had been expecting this.

The man patted the dog on the head – presumably to illustrate affection? – before placing one hand on each muscular knee and heaving himself up from the bench, releasing an unexpectedly loud groan as he did so. He underwent a series of quick but deliberate stretches; I half-expected the animal to do the same.

'Come on then, girl.'

He gave a tug on the chain-link lead. When they moved to leave the park, I moved to follow.

The dog walked two steps ahead, pulling the lead taut as animals are inclined to. But it soon forced out a coughing fit. They paused and the owner lowered himself down, voicing concern for his pet.

I had stayed a measured twenty paces behind them since leaving the park, but this break in their stride disturbed me. I could have turned in the other direction and made my escape, or I could have continued walking, moved straight past them. But instead, I intervened.

'That sounds like a nasty cough.'

The dog was enduring enthusiastic throat rubs from its owner. Its eyes had narrowed into slits and small grumbles were now rising from its throat in place of the cough.

'She never learns, do you, Peaches? Say no, Pops, I never learn, and I never listen to my pops when he tells me that I shouldn't pull on the lead.'

His language deteriorated into something that I had previously heard referred to as baby talk; this seemed to be something that animal lovers employed on a regular basis. The dog appeared to be enjoying the whole thing – I made a mental note of it for future reference – and as a result was now making determined attempts to lick the man's face. He repeatedly dodged her advances. Baby talk was one thing, but kisses were clearly too much.

I watched their display and, just for a second, I wondered: Who would miss them?

'Christ, how rude of me.'

He pushed himself into an upright position as he spoke; by the time his legs were fully extended he was at least six inches taller than me. He would be incredibly hard to subdue.

'I'm Paul, and this mutt is Peaches.'

One hand remained wrapped around the end of the dog's lead as he spoke, while the other was buried inside his front left pocket. I was grateful that he had skipped the handshake.

'I thought you were Pops?'

He laughed and I took this as a cue to smile.

'Guilty as charged. I am one of those embarrassing animal-loving types who believes that their pet is their child. Ergo, I am Peaches' pops.' He followed this with another laugh; it felt awkward to flash another smile but I wasn't sure how else to continue. 'Honestly, it's a more common affliction than you might realise.'

'I believe you.'

'Anyway, thank you – Christ, how rude of me again, I didn't even get your name.' He laughed again. This one was awkward, embarrassed. 'I promise that I am usually much better at this conversation malarkey.'

'I'm Gillian.'

'Well thank you, Gillian, for stopping to check on this silly mutt of mine.'

The dog let out a disgruntled moan that was timed so perfectly I wondered whether their conversations were rehearsed.

'Peaches and I are heading up this way. Are you–'

'Oh, I'm up this way as well,' I lied. By now I was already a forty-five-minute walk away from home.

Paul and Peaches lived an additional ten minutes of walking in the opposite direction, and Paul was a conversation enthusiast. During those ten minutes I discovered a little about him: single, freelance website designer, Prescott Lane.

'It's a recent move, actually. Nasty break-up – you've probably heard that romantic little tune a thousand times, right?'

Faerie Tale Theatre. 1987. Lesley Ann Warren. 'There's more to life than romance.' I offered him a smile and nodded, hoping for a convincing expression.

'She kept custody of the house; I got custody of the dog.'

Peaches' backstory sounded almost as downtrodden as that of her owner. She had apparently been abandoned outside a shelter at four months old, covered in various cuts and scrapes. She was adopted by Paul who had treated her like 'a four-legged queen' in the five years that he had owned her. I made a special effort to 'Aww' in what felt like the right places.

'This is where we get off I'm afraid. Peaches and I are in the park the same time most days, so perhaps we'll all bump into each other again.'

I gave Paul my best smile before saying my goodbyes to both him and Peaches.

'It's been a real pleasure,' I said. And I meant it.

Chapter nine

There isn't much in this world that you can't get, as long as you're willing to pay for it. Which would perhaps explain why my mother – just thirty-five hours after leaving – was calling to tell me she'd managed to get an emergency therapy appointment for me, with a woman based just ten minutes from our house. She gave me the details slowly, sounding out each syllable as though talking to a hard-of-hearing child. And another eighteen hours or so later, I was working up a draft of which guts I was allowed, or expected, to spill to this new woman in my life.

I felt what might have been nerves – or maybe apprehension – on the journey to the therapist's office. In the hope that I could delay the appointment for as long as possible, I even opted to walk rather than drive. But, standing outside the main entrance to the building, the therapist-to-patient confrontation suddenly seemed unavoidable. The appointment room itself was fairly unremarkable. I'm not sure what I'd been expecting of the interior of the woman's office space, but it seemed too simple by comparison to her ornate personal exterior. Her hair was pulled back into a perfect – compulsively neat, some might say – ponytail that sat dead centre at the back of her head; it made a pendulum of itself as I followed her from the reception area to her office, so captivating that I was almost saddened when she turned to face me. Her clothes weren't impressive on their own – an expertly pressed black blouse coupled with darker-than-navy blue jeans – but they worked to give her a casual look. Which, given this potentially vulnerable (for me) situation, I thought might have been a deliberate effort on her part. On entering the office, she steered me away from the professional desk, and the high-backed chairs that were positioned around it, encouraging me instead towards the two sofas that sat opposite each other at the other end of the room. The door had hidden them – although I couldn't say whether this was accidental or strategic – when I'd first walked in. Between the two sofas there sat a low coffee table that held a jug of water and two squat glasses. I wondered how often those tumblers were changed.

'Please, help yourself.'

She had caught me looking. I held up my hand and shook my head as she continued to skim through a small selection of papers. This was only our opening consultation; how much information could she possibly have already, and why had my mother provided it?

'Before we get started, Gillian, is there anything that you want to ask me?'

'What's your name?'

The woman tutted quietly, at herself, I assumed, as I could see nothing tut-worthy in what I'd asked her. There was a very real possibility that I should already know her name, that it was something my mother might have told me during her initial reveal of the appointment. But the information had tumbled out somewhere between then and now.

'I'm Louise.' *Doesn't ring a bell,* I thought. She leaned forward as she spoke, holding her hand in an appropriate pre-shake position, despite us already having completed this formality five minutes earlier. I reciprocated the gesture before falling hard against the back of the sofa. 'Quite rude of me, Gillian, my apologies. It's been a long old day.'

I nodded, smiled. I was unsure of what to say.

'We'll get started then?' she said.

'Okay.'

'I have a few introductory questions here, if that's okay with you.'

I nodded, again.

'In your own words, Gillian, why are you here today?'

'My mother told me that I needed to be.'

A small laugh erupted from her as she made a note of something on her pad. When she glanced back to me, she found my deadpan expression looking back at her.

'Oh.' She crossed out whatever she had just written. 'Okay, and is that because she thinks that there's something to be gained from this, do you think?'

'Or she just wanted to rob me of an hour of my afternoon.' I punctuated the line with a tight smile, to soften the blow.

'Okay, different phrasing then. Why do you think that your mother wants you to be here today? A serious answer.'

There was a window to my left. It was too inconvenient a distance away to observe anything specific outside, but it was certainly close enough to gaze through while putting my answer together.

'My father has recently passed away, under difficult circumstances, especially difficult, I mean, and I think my mother is concerned that I'm not handling the whole thing as I should be.'

'And how should someone handle the death of a parent?'

I searched for a point of reference: *Bambi*? A little juvenile. *Batman*? A little too honourable.

'I'm glad that you've stalled on that, Gillian, because you're illustrating my point for me. There are no shoulds when we lose someone who is close to us, so I'd like to put that word itself on the back-burner for now?' Her heavy inflexion made a question of the sentence. I nodded a quick confirmation and she continued. 'Okay, good.' She added something to her notes before setting the pen and paper down on the stretch of sofa alongside her. 'You said that your father died under especially difficult circumstances. Maybe you can tell me something more about what you mean by that?'

There was more, much more, but I momentarily wobbled over which version of events I should offer her. I had walked for at least forty minutes to attend this appointment. This woman was far enough from my own neighbourhood for my father's death to have missed the area's idle gossip. But still, she was one Internet search away from verifying the whole story.

'There was an accident at home. My father was something of a drunk.'

As soon as the words popped out I was shaking my head at them. I was inexplicably flustered, but I knew that those sentences didn't fit together – at least, not without something else sandwiched in between them.

'Take your time, Gillian. There's no rush.'

But there was. Mum had only paid for an hour.

Determinedly, I started again: 'My father was an alcoholic, and physically abusive towards my mother. One evening they had a drunken altercation and my mother tried to defend herself and, I suppose because my father didn't exactly have his full wits about him, I don't know, something that would have been a harmless shove under normal circumstances just became something more fatal.' I shook my head at my own phrasing. 'Not that there are degrees of fatality, obviously.'

Louise flashed a sympathetic smile. 'And when did this happen?'

'It's been seven weeks and four days.'

'That's very precise, Gillian.'

I wasn't sure what I was expected to say to that.

'I have to be precise,' I replied.

Louise gave a quick nod as she reached for the pen and paper from her side. She wedged the paper against her left thigh, angled in such a way that I could see nothing of what she was writing. I wondered what I'd said that was noteworthy.

'Have you always had to be precise, or is that a recent habit?'

It felt like there was an unspoken section of the sentence but, try as I might, I couldn't find it. I turned it over for six seconds and after that it felt not only polite but absolutely necessary that I say something in response. Louise sat with one leg crossed over the other and her hands slightly parted, as if physically braced to catch my answer.

'Yes, I've always had to be.'

She paused, scribbled, and picked up her speech again. 'It's still very early days, Gillian. Both you and your mother are very much in the infant stages of this process; not that it's an exact science, of course. But given that there's no timeline for this, it's important that you unpack some of the feelings you're having, so we can really get to grips with this stage, you see? I'd really like your own thoughts on this. Because you must have some, Gillian, maybe even some that you've been keeping from your mother?'

Entirely by accident, my right eyebrow had arched midway through her speech, which was, I thought, likely to be the reason behind her final words of encouragement. Perhaps she was right; perhaps I did have some thoughts about the whole mess. Unfortunately she was also right about my unwavering reluctance to reveal those thoughts to anyone else, which saw us sink into a solid minute-long silence while I considered my options with more panic than I was accustomed to feeling. What was I meant to say here versus what was I allowed to say here? That I was angry, disappointed? That in all my wildest fantasies not once had I imagined such a crushing anticlimax? That the only thing I missed when it came to my father was the opportunity to get rid of him more effectively – dare I say, more enjoyably?

'You can be honest here, Gillian.'

But not that honest, I thought.

'I feel angry.'

'At your mother, or your father?'

I hadn't realised that I was allowed to be angry with either of them, specifically, but rather just the situation as a whole. I tried another thought on for size: 'At both of them, I think.'

'Because?'

Because he died too quickly? Because she took the credit for it?

'Because they're my parents and they should have done things better.' A heavy sigh fell from Louise to punctuate my answer and, for a second, I was flustered by the thought that it perhaps hadn't been a believable one. 'That sounds childish, I know–'

'It sounds reasonable, Gillian.' Interruptions typically irked me but this one felt like a salvation. 'Our parents love and support us, and we rely on them for that. When that natural order becomes disturbed, we're allowed to not feel okay about it, and you are certainly allowed to feel angry. I wouldn't encourage you to hold that anger in, either.'

There was a twinge of something in my stomach. 'You wouldn't?'

'Absolutely not. There are stages, Gillian, and if you stall at one then all you do is stop yourself from moving on to whatever comes next, which just creates an entirely new problem in itself. Do you understand that?'

I thought I did, yes. I nodded.

'I'd like us to talk a little more about your father, if that's okay with you? You said that he was physically abusive to your mother. Just to your mother?'

This was a line of questioning that I should have anticipated, really.

Do you remember when it started?
Were you always aware of it?
Did it happen often?
To what extent was he violent?

And so, I answered – 'Yes, just my mother' – and all of the questions that followed, until we hit on an entirely new area of questioning. A notably more difficult one, in fact.

'And how does that make you feel about your mother?'

'I'm sorry?'

'Presumably it had an impact on your relationship with her?'

Had it? Did it? How would I even know? I spat out several false starts before grabbing at a thread that I felt comfortable pulling.

'It may have done but I don't really have a wider point of reference for that.'

She nodded, scribbled, spoke: 'Okay then, how would you describe your relationship with your mother?'

By the time I was seven years old my numeracy and literacy skills belonged to someone two years my senior. I was pushed

– by teachers, never by family – to excel academically in both English and Mathematics, and this encouragement didn't waver until I was twelve. Then Mr Burton noted my natural aptitude for the sciences – biology in particular – and after that my efforts switched subjects. In one field or another, at one time or another, I have always been of above average intelligence. So what was so goddamn difficult about Louise's question? My relationship with my father had been so temperamental, beginning as far back as I could recall, that my quiet and understated relationship with my mother had always felt satisfactory enough to me, normal enough to me – by comparison, that is. It was a new thought – a troubling thought, I'll admit – that my relationship with my mother may actually be below par as well, by a different comparison.

Noting that she had thrown something of a spanner into my internal workings, Louise said: 'Gillian, we've done a lot of work for one session. Maybe we should save this for the next time I see you?' She paused, for confirmation I assumed. I smiled, more in response to her presupposition that she would see me again, and she continued: 'Rachel can set you up with another appointment now, or you can phone her another time, maybe when you've had some time to digest the things from today?'

'I'd like to discuss things with my mother, really.'

It was, of course, a complete lie. I had no idea why I'd even said it.

'Of course. Whatever you're more comfortable with.' As she spoke she walked to her desk. She returned holding an off-white business card. 'Bear in mind, Gillian, that I haven't met your mother. However, from what we've discussed today, this may be useful.' She handed me the card.

Alison Warren.

'Alison runs an outreach programme for people who have or have been in…' She paused, searching for the most appropriate phrase. 'Difficult relationships, of varying degrees. It may be useful for your mother to get in touch with her.'

I slipped the card into the back pocket of my jeans and thanked Louise, for both the business card and for her time – my mother had paid perfectly good money for the luxury of both things, despite my not wanting either of them. Louise saw me out of her office and – inappropriately, I thought – said that she looked forward to seeing me again.

We shook hands then, said our goodbyes, and I left the building, already drafting a number of perfectly feasible excuses to explain to my mother why I wouldn't ever be going back.

Chapter ten

I was far from being a committed fan of social media. It had always seemed disingenuous to call strangers friends and to share your emotional innards with them through the medium of an Internet connection. What recent information could I even have shared with my primary school comrades and undergraduate associates?

Getting ready for Dad's funeral – feeling sad ☹
Had to help mum get dressed again today - awkward much?!

Nevertheless, I did have one social media account attached to my name, for the sake of maintaining an acceptable public persona. And so, for an average of five minutes per week, I devoted some concentrated time to the maintenance of a digital profile that I strongly resented having.

Three days after my mother left, the day after I had met Paul the dog walker, I typed my sign-in details into the log-in window and waited for a flood of information to arrive on my laptop screen. I already knew that I would be interested in little to none of it. Of everything that you could find online now, rifling through old friend's unmentionables seemed like a thorough waste of a broadband connection. However, that day, when my information loaded, there was a message I couldn't recall seeing before hovering at the top of the page.

One new request for friendship: Daniel Lodge
(You have no mutual friends in common. If you do not know Daniel, please click here.)

He had tricked me, I now saw. I didn't know this man as Daniel Lodge, although he was undeniably *the* Daniel, but despite his frequent pleas for my last name during dinner, he had neglected to provide me with his own – and now I understood why. It was tempting to lie then; to say that no, I didn't know Daniel Lodge, and to let the Internet cleanly sweep this character out of my life. The compact picture in the window alongside his name was undoubtedly him; from the small slip of his shoulders visible in the bottom corners of the image, I thought he may have even been wearing the same jacket. His mouth was contorted into the same lopsided smile and I wondered then whose benefit this was for: the camera maybe, or perhaps the person behind it. Despite my initial irritation, I felt compelled to click on this smaller window to enlarge the picture, and it quickly hijacked the majority of my laptop screen.

His expression was familiar now. I might have been looking in on a friend who I had known for some time, rather than a stranger. I clicked the screen in the appropriate area to scroll across to another photograph and there he was again, sporting the exact same smile as if it were a default setting. In this picture there was a friend either side of him, and a slightly smaller sag of skin beneath his chin than there had been in the previous photograph. This second picture was three years older and I developed a sudden need, on seeing this time stamp, to know what had happened between then and now, aside from a small amount of weight gain.

I clicked my way out of the album and back towards the request. I still felt a measured amount of apprehension but it felt miniscule in comparison to my curiosity about precisely what could happen next. And so, I clicked ACCEPT.

Gillian Thompson is now friends with Daniel Lodge.
To view Daniel's profile, please click here.

I now felt contractually obliged, by the Gods of social media, to suffer any and all consequences associated with my decision. And then the first consequence arrived.

You have one new chat window open.
Daniel Lodge:
Do you come here often?
Haha
Seriously though GT, you know how to keep a man waiting
It's been three whole days
I thought I might have just imagined you

He was a multiple-messager. One of the worst types of messager you could encounter. The weight of my decision to accept his request felt heavier now, which was irrational, really, given that I could escape the conversation whenever I needed to by clicking the cross in the corner.

However, in amongst these feelings, there was also a small flutter of what I thought was probably excitement at the prospect of replying, matched only by the flutter of nerves at not quite knowing what to say.

'I don't come here a lot, no,' I said aloud in time with my typing the message. The response felt bland, curt, two sides that I didn't particularly want to display so soon. I backspaced, returned to Daniel's stream of messages for a second read-through, and tried my very best to land somewhere in the region of charming:

Gillian Thompson:
How do you know that you didn't imagine me?

I felt that I had drafted a perfectly acceptable response but when the reply floated up on the screen I realised it had sounded much better in my mind than in practice. I should have read it aloud, I thought.

Daniel Lodge:
Then how am I talking to you now?
Unless this is all an elaborate hallucination

Are there no depths that I won't sink to – just to talk to a pretty girl?

I couldn't recall a time before this when I had been referred to as pretty. Pretty peculiar, pretty unusual, pretty fucking weird by my father during one of his drunken displays, but no one had ever thought of me as just pretty. Before I could muster an appropriate response I started to suffer a disconcerting physiological one somewhere in my lower abdomen.

Daniel Lodge:
And yes. I think you're pretty. Is that okay?

Gillian Thompson:
I'm not sure.

Daniel Lodge:
Oh
Well
It was kind of a rhetorical question anyway

Gillian Thompson:
I'm sorry. I'm usually quite good at spotting those.

We maintained a virtual exchange for some twenty-eight minutes after this but despite my well-drafted responses I still felt nervous. While the distance created by the computer screen lent me more thinking time, it also took away the facial expressions and intonations of Daniel's responses, which made him impossible to read. There were no narrowed eyes, no dipped smiles, no half-laughs, and in their absence I felt unprepared to hold a conversation at all.

Daniel didn't ask any more rhetorical questions – I don't think – but he did pursue the usual topics, asking how I was (fine, thank you) and what I had been doing with myself since our encounter (nothing exciting, I'm afraid). This avenue of conversation was a safer area, and a relatively familiar one. I knew that it was proper to enquire how he was now, and perhaps even how life had been treating him.

Daniel Lodge:
Ah, fit as a fiddle on the outside
To be honest though
I've got quite a lot going at the moment
Some stuff on my mind

That was as much information as he offered. I wasn't sure whether the natural pause that followed was something I should fill with questions, or pleas for further details. Or even whether there was an expectation that I should want further details. Speaking out loud, I tried on various options:

'What's going on?'

'Tell me all about it.'

'What is it that's on your mind then?'

I couldn't make any of them fit comfortably, and for the first time during our exchange I felt grateful that it was being constructed through a computer screen. When three small dancing dots appeared in the corner of the window to indicate Daniel was typing, I felt even further gratitude.

Daniel Lodge:
My aunt went into hospital this morning

Gillian Thompson:
I'm really sorry to hear that!

I added the exclamation mark to highlight how sorry I really was.

Without further information it felt tricky to react beyond what I had already said. Daniel had led me to believe that his aunt was quite ill, and that her cancer showed no signs of shrinking. I assumed that this meant she was a frequent visitor to the hospital, which would surely make this latest visit an unremarkable thing. But it seemed to bother Daniel more than an unremarkable thing should.

Daniel Lodge:
They found this thing on her last scan
Something that wasn't there before
And so they think things might be getting worse

Terminal, I thought. *They think it might be terminal.* But Daniel didn't want to say that. Recent months had taught me that people had quite an aversion to acknowledging mortality.

Daniel Lodge:
They've decided the best option is to open her up
Have a look around
See if they can find out more that way

I didn't need facial expressions or vocal intonations to confirm that Daniel was upset by this development. And, strangely, I found Daniel's upset to be quite upsetting myself. Another virtual silence appeared and, after so much effort on Daniel's part, I assumed that this time I would have to fuel the conversation. I relied on my limited experience and on borrowed sentimentality:

Gillian Thompson:
Is there anything that I can do to better the situation?

As I said the sentence aloud to myself, I couldn't help but wince. The sentiment was right but the expression was rigid. I was grateful again for the computer screen. Although I had typed and sent the words, they just didn't sound right coming out in my own voice.

Daniel Lodge:
There is one thing
If you don't mind
And if that was a sincere offer
Because you can never tell over these things
Haha

There was something admirable about his honesty and I felt moved to match it when it came to my reply. I quickly typed a response – 'I'm sorry, no, that wasn't actually said with sincerity; I was just trying to be polite' – but I knew that it wasn't right. As I read and reread the message, I began to develop a sense of uncertainty – that no, I should not be doing this. The tip of my right index finger hovered about in the small space between the backspace button and the enter key. I eventually settled on the former and tapped at it repeatedly, deleting one callous character at a time. I typed what felt like a more socially acceptable message and hit enter without even proofreading it, for fear that I might delete this one, too:

Gillian Thompson:
Of course. I wouldn't have extended the offer otherwise.

The response was a little clinical, again, but it was certainly more approachable than the previous attempt. And while I read and reread this message, waiting for a reply – or at least the dancing dots that would indicate a reply was on its way – a thought occurred to me that I found unsettling: did everyone have to try this hard? Of course, it wasn't exactly the first time that this thought had made an appearance. Throughout years of self-editing and linguistic censorship in even the most simple of conversations, I had thought this before. But now, observing the awkward tone of my own messages sat alongside the perfect ease of Daniel's, I couldn't help but pull myself back to the question. I wondered then whether this was more difficult because it was with Daniel. I couldn't see what was so different about him, but there must have been something. Throughout my entire teenage years people had failed to hold my attention for particularly long stretches of time, but Daniel?

And before that thought progressed further, a message interrupted me:

Daniel Lodge:
Are you free this afternoon?
I know that it's short notice
But something about being here at the house
While she's in there
I just need to get out for a while I think
But I understand if you're busy
Or even if you just don't want to haha

Despite Daniel's virtual laugh, I couldn't envisage him laughing in person. The only image that I could scramble together was one of Daniel sitting in an empty house, waiting for the dancing dots to appear on his screen.

The clock that was tucked into the bottom left of my laptop screen reminded me I was busy – 'Peaches and I are in the park the same time most days' – and I did have somewhere to be, fairly soon. But something else seemed determined to convince me again that that wasn't a proper response and so I endeavoured to strike a balance between easing Daniel's apparent emotional discomfort, and inflicting any type of discomfort on myself.

Gillian Thompson:
Do you know The Runner's Route park?

Daniel Lodge:
On the way to town?
Where the dog walkers go?

Gillian Thomson:
Yes. That's the one. It's a nice place to spend an afternoon.

I asked Daniel if he could meet me at the park in thirty minutes. Paul and Peaches were less likely to bump into us then, but we'd still be in good time to see them both.

Chapter eleven

Daniel and I spent the afternoon walking. In terms of actual time it was no longer than an hour and thirty-two minutes, but Daniel's tendency to fill every silence gave me the impression that our walk had lasted longer – despite my multiple attempts to further amuse myself with several rounds of 'spot the dog walker'. When the trail came to an end I hoped that this would provide an opportunity for our conversation to conclude as well.

'Ah, course, Gillian must have a whole clan of Thompsons waiting for her at home.'

'I just live with my mother.'

'Ah.'

The silence lasted a beat too long; I had to fill it.

'She's actually away at the moment, but all that means is that the task of keeping the house clean falls on me. So that's my occupation for the rest of the day.'

It was a flimsy excuse but I hoped that it would be believable enough to explain why I couldn't commit any more time to Daniel. And sure enough, it worked. But Daniel was right when he said that I wouldn't need to clean the house every day. And yes, I suppose everyone did need to eat at some point. And yes, there really is something special about a home-cooked meal, isn't there? And, of course, I had a number that he could reach me on. And before I really knew what was happening I was typing my home telephone number into the keypad of Daniel's mobile. He said that he would call me the following morning to see what time he should arrive and whether he could do anything to assist.

Bring whatever you expect to eat, I wanted to say. But instead I told him that I looked forward to hearing from him – and the words actually felt right.

At 9:32 the following morning I was preoccupied with the mammoth task of filling the silence in the house by making a noisy breakfast. The kettle wobbled as it approached boiling point, its whistle becoming more pronounced, and then the unfamiliar tone of our house phone leaked in from the hallway. It took longer than it should have done for me to register the sound.

'Hello?'

'Hi, Gillian?'

'Yes, it's Gillian. Daniel?'

I hadn't been expecting a phone call from anyone else, but there was something attractive about pretending that I was. People like to know that they are hankering after something popular.

'Yes! I thought I might have missed you; the phone seemed to be ringing forever. I'm glad I that I have caught you, because I've been thinking about our plans.'

I felt the return of an unsettling knot inside my stomach that somehow seemed to encapsulate my general feelings towards Daniel. I was already becoming quite accustomed to the push (I wonder if he's calling to cancel the whole dreadful thing) and the pull (wouldn't that be disappointing?).

'It's pretty unfair of me to invite myself over like that and then expect you to do all the cooking. And I am after all a fairly modern, respectable, metro sort of man, I think.'

He deliberately paused, waiting for some kind of denial or confirmation of what he had just said. I wasn't sure which to give.

'Okay, or not – ah, so my suggestion. Maybe I could come over to yours and I can be in charge of cooking? You'll just need to point me in the direction of the kitchen when I get there, and relax. And maybe sort out something for dessert, if you can manage it.' He laughed.

'Why?'

'Why what?'

'Why would you do that?'

'Oh, just to be nice, Gillian. You know, to be nice to you.'

I didn't quite understand but I gave him the address anyway.

***

I was halfway to the supermarket's in-store bakery later that day when I saw him – Paul, that is, not Daniel – with an empty basket hung over his arm. Strategically placing myself at the end of the snack aisle, I watched him head towards what turned out to be the pet section. I hovered, pretending to peruse the discounted savoury items that had been conveniently displayed at the end of every other aisle, giving me ample opportunity to linger. Barely ten seconds had passed when I eyed Paul again, and saw that he was torn between a soft plastic pig and a packet of tennis balls. He dropped the latter into his basket before his fingers pulsed around the pig, forcing out three sharp squeaks. There must have been something pleasing about the noise because he dropped that in too. We very nearly bumped into each other during our respective food shops; not that Paul noticed. Fresh vegetables and fruit, followed by meat, and then the unavoidable frozen items – because even the most health-conscious shopper sometimes buys for convenience. He made a last-minute dash to the bakery section, reminding me of why I'd come to the supermarket in the first instance; had the circumstances been different, I would have thanked him for this. I still hadn't chosen a dessert. Paul picked up a large tiger loaf and balanced it on top of the weeks' worth of shopping crammed into the basket. He left me struggling between pecan plaits and cinnamon swirls. Tuesday seemed an odd day for a weekly food shop.

The rest of the day proved uneventful, that is until Daniel arrived at 6:28pm (earlier than he had told me he would be there, but it seemed petty to mention it). After I opened the door, I made two conclusions about Daniel's character: his lopsided facial expression definitely was a default setting, and that hideous corduroy jacket was his favourite article of clothing. In two hands he held a total of three plastic carrier bags, all of which looked strained with the weight of Daniel's food purchases. His smile was now framed by inflated cheeks, puffed out in exasperation. He took hesitant steps forward, struggling with the weight of his purchases. Each movement was accompanied by the rustle of plastic – a threat that the bags may not make it to the kitchen. Unsure of my responsibilities, I stepped to the side of the front door to allow him access and directed him towards the kitchen.

'Through the dining room, towards that far door.'

Daniel nodded and continued his weighted walk from one side of the house to the other. On arriving at the closed door he turned to angle the ball of his shoulder against the wood; he heaved his weight against it then struggled to keep upright as the door gave way beneath him with considerable ease. A stampede of sounds followed his entrance and just as I was beginning to imagine a cavalcade of meat and vegetables making their escape across the floor, I heard a not entirely convincing, 'I'm okay.'

'Is it safe to come in?'

'Absolutely, GT, abso-bloody-lutely.'

Inside the room there was a picture of calm that left me wondering whether the previous crashes and bangs had been theatrical. The kitchen work surface was now a display of disorganised colour as Daniel had carefully removed each vegetable and arranged them in a system that failed to make sense to me, but almost certainly made sense to him.

'You haven't jumped ship to vegetarianism or anything drastic like that, have you?' he asked, still busying himself with preparations.

'No, definitely not.'

'Marvellous. Because, Gillian Thompson, you are about to have the best bit of meat that you can get in this town. And trust me, I've done the legwork to find the best bit of meat today, I can promise you that much. I kept asking around for a butcher – a town like this must have a butcher – but everyone kept mentioning the same shutdown shop, like that's any use. Something about the owner dying?'

Daniel was concentrating on the piece of meat, manoeuvring it around in the limited space between the hot tap and the kitchen sink. He was facing away from me while doing this, so he couldn't have seen my facial expression. He couldn't know that shop now technically belonged to me and my mother. I didn't know whether, in light of recent revelations, I was now obliged to tell him.

'That's my father's shop. Sorry – it was.'

The meat hit the metal sink with an unappetising thud.

'Oh, arses.' He turned to look at me; his hands dripped blood-tinged water on to the floor. 'Gillian, I–'

'It's okay,' I said. 'But I don't want to talk about it.'

Daniel banished me from the kitchen after that. My involvement in the preparation was limited to locating the necessary pots and pans and preparing the dinner table; the latter being a job that I couldn't remember being given the responsibility of before. I set out place settings and crept into the kitchen to find the necessary cutlery. I could hear my mother's voice throughout the whole process. *This dining table will be kept for the best, love – only for very special occasions.* The words had been riddled with pride and admiration for the beautiful table and accompanying chairs. She said them without a hint of irony or humour, as if she hadn't realised that the best actually wasn't yet to come.

Somehow nearly forty minutes had passed by in this nostalgia when the sound of Daniel kicking his way out of the kitchen interrupted me. He wandered into the room with an air of confidence that didn't fit him, a food-laden plate precariously balanced on each hand. He set one plate down in front of me and took the other to his own place setting at the opposite end of the room. He stood at the head of the table with one hand pressed against his chest and his head cocked slightly towards the ceiling; he released a dramatic cough before he began speaking, in an accent that didn't belong to him. ''Ere we have le pork, salted and seasoned on a bed of peppered vegetablay mash accompanied by twice roasteed potatoes. Bon appétit, madam!'

He made what I thought was meant to be a kissing sound before collapsing into his chair and grabbing his cutlery. His cheeks were red and his hair more dishevelled.

'I'm starving,' he said.

His voice had reverted to the default sound, but I had to ask: 'Why were you talking like that?'

'Because the best chefs are French, *oui*?'

'Are you one of the best chefs?'

'I've given you twice roasteed potatoes; how can you even ask me that?' He finished the sentence with a wink that I hadn't seen him use before, but I thought that it suited him. After that we ate, we laughed, and the potatoes really were delicious.

It was the closest that the house and its inhabitants had ever come to hosting a conventionally normal evening – with a guest too! As we began to clean up from dinner I wondered whether my mother would be proud of the evening's performance. *Look, Mum, I'm a real live girl; isn't this what you wanted?*

'You should stay sitting while I fetch dessert,' I said, thinking that this was a successful attempt at being an exemplary host.

I had purchased two sizeable cinnamon swirls, which I served alongside a scoop of vanilla ice cream. It had taken longer than I had expected to decide on an appropriate dessert. I hadn't realised before that I cared quite so much about the distinct differences between plaits and swirls. Daniel seemed to enjoy my choice. He delivered a series of overdramatised 'Oohs' and 'Ahhs' before leaning back and rubbing his stomach.

'Was that homemade?'

'They told me that it was when I bought it.'

Daniel released a small chuckle. 'Gillian Thompson, you do make me laugh.'

'I don't mean to.'

'I think that's precisely the reason why you do.'

'So you're really just laughing at me?'

'Yes, Gillian, but in a very kind way.'

'I don't think that I understand.'

'I don't think that you need to.'

Daniel sat opposite me, smiling, with a much more severe facial imbalance than I had seen before. The left side of his mouth was now tucked up in such a half-smile that his left eye was near to closing.

'You look happy,' I observed.

'Oh, GT, I am much more than happy. I am content.'

A Single Man. 2009. Colin Firth. 'The dumbest creatures are always the happiest.' I tried to smile as I shook the reference away; Daniel was hardly dumb, as far as I could gather.

After this he offered to assist with the cleaning of pots, pans, and other utensils, but I was reluctant to let him after he had already given so much effort to the evening. Instead I pointed him in the direction of the living room.

'It'll take hours to do all of that on your own,' he said, in a tone that suggested he was trying to reason with me.

'You're welcome to make yourself comfortable, or leave.' It was the first time that I had been so aware of my own bluntness. 'I didn't mean that how I think it may have sounded.' It was also the first time that I had felt a pang of guilt for it.

'It's okay, I understand what you meant.'

We went our separate ways into the living room and the kitchen, and I was surprised to see that Daniel's estimation of how long it would take to clean up was far from hyperbolic. I hadn't even been aware that this amount of cooking paraphernalia inhabited our kitchen. It would be much more time-effective, I thought, for me to cook next time. Or perhaps next time we could go for dinner somewhere, given the relative success of our previous encounter at a restaurant. And sandwiched somewhere between those thoughts – and the uncharacteristic thoughts that followed – I realised that I had just decided that I would like to see Daniel again. It was an odd sensation, like heat spreading somewhere in my lower abdomen, and I had to drop the half-clean plate back into the bowl of water to properly concentrate on what I was feeling.

Star Trek: Voyager. 1995. Jennifer Lien. 'Romance is not a malfunction.' Exhaling, I thought: *so, this is romance then?*

Chapter twelve

After Daniel left the house, my mother called so promptly that I actually managed to convince myself she must have known he'd been there. She mentioned nothing, of course. But the human mind works in mysterious ways. She called to verify that I was coping – which I was – and to ask what I'd been doing with myself – not much. Three careful questions followed about my day-to-day life, and she skirted around the issue of whether I had been to my therapy appointment. Sifting through my experiments box while my mother worked up to this apparently impossible question, I eventually settled on a jarred heart, surrounded by tiny pieces of tissue. I shook the container from side to side and watched the flecks tumble down to the bottom as the liquid settled.

'Louise is nice,' I finally said. She sighed, which I took to be a marker of relief.

'The appointment went okay, then?' She tried to sound casual, like she hadn't steered the conversation in this direction.

I provided her with a brief overview of the meeting – strategically removing the discussion of my inadequate parents – and said yes, it had gone okay, and yes, I would see Louise again if she wanted me to.

'Gillian, what's that noise in the background?'

'I'm sorry?'

'There's a noise, like water or something.'

With over-baked care I lowered the jar back into the box.

'I can't hear anything, Mum. It must just be interference on your end.'

We said our farewells shortly after; the fabricated interference had given us both a good enough excuse. The next morning when she called again, it was to ask whether I would mind being left alone for another few days. I thought of the new man – men – in my life, of the time that I could freely spend with them.

'No, Mum,' I said. 'Whatever it is you need.'

It turned out that it wasn't quite the unencumbered span of time I had expected it to be. My mother continued to call intermittently over the days that followed, at random intervals which made her intrusions impossible to predict, and I began to think she may be trying to catch me out on something. Throughout my adolescence she had always resisted asking questions – about my whereabouts, my after-school activities, any friends that I may have accumulated. She was always giving me space – perhaps too much space, in hindsight – to have my own privacy. Now it felt like she was somehow trying to compensate for that. It wasn't until midway through our fourth impromptu phone call that I wondered why I didn't just tell her about Daniel; why I had decided to make a secret of him. Listening to my inner adolescent – the one that observed and mimicked, rather than the one who poisoned animals – I decided: it was nice to have something that was just mine.

Daniel and I saw each other every day during the week my mother was away. It didn't even feel like a conscious decision – not on my part, at least – but rather something that just happened. It didn't occur to me that eventually my mother would come home and could, quite easily, in fact, complicate our relationship – assuming that's what Daniel and I had fallen into. So it was somewhat jarring when, following an afternoon with Daniel, I came home to find my mother perched on the edge of my father's armchair in the living room. Her elbows were propped on her knees, allowing one hand to hang down somewhere between her thighs, while the other lingered about in the area of her neck. I watched her with curiosity as one hand drifted up to her chin, creating what looked like a parody of The Thinker.

'Mum?'

She looked away from whatever had been holding her attention and stared straight at me. 'Love, where have you been?'

'I've been with Daniel.'

The words fell out before I could censor them. I'd had no idea just how desperate I'd been to talk about him. And yet there his name was, perched on the tip of my tongue, just waiting for me to open my mouth.

'Who's Daniel?'

'A friend, I think.'

'You think?'

'It's a hard question to answer, Mum.'

'Only because you're making it hard, Gillian.'

She had brought a newfound confidence home with her, and I wasn't sure that I liked it. 'Can I go to the toilet before we have this conversation?'

She sighed and nodded with some effort, as if I were asking her for something more inconvenient than the chance to empty my bladder. Dodging the bathroom, I instead headed to my bedroom – my safe haven – to buy myself enough time to process the updated mother sitting downstairs. But as soon as I stepped through the doorway I was hit by a smell that didn't belong there. The acidity of vomit combined with an undercurrent of bleach.

Back downstairs, I hoped to strike up a reasonably normal conversation.

'How was your time with Jackie?'

There was certainly something different about her. The trousers she wore – which I didn't think belonged to her – were carefully pressed with designer creases, while her shirt – another garment that I didn't recognise – was deliberately oversized in a way that made her frame look even more petite than it had done previously. Her hair, too, was different, cared for, and her make-up had a professional touch to it, although the colour distinction between her jawline and neck was enough to make me wince.

She seemed uninterested in discussing her time with Jackie, and instead served up the bare minimum of details. It was nice, she said, to spend some time with her sister after being apart for so long, but she never seemed to venture further.

'You must have enjoyed yourself to want to stay longer.'

'Oh, I was fine while I was away, yes, love.'

I ignored the implications of this, hoping that I could wedge another question into our dialogue before my mother could take hold of the conversation. But she beat me to the punch.

'Now, tell me about this Daniel. When did you meet him?'

'That evening that I went for a stroll, out to the park, before you left.' I felt the need to keep adding to my explanation although I had nothing else to give her. 'That's when I met him.'

'You didn't mention it?'

'It didn't seem worth mentioning, really.'

With pursed lips she nodded at this, before shifting her tongue around her mouth in a movement that made it look like she were physically chewing.

'And what are your intentions with him?'

'My intentions?'

She pulled her mouth up at the corner as one eyebrow arched several millimetres higher than the other to make a new expression – one that seemed to suggest I should know exactly what she was talking about. I remained quiet for what my mother obviously thought was a beat too long and so she continued: 'Gillian, you weren't going to do anything to him, were you? Hurt him, I mean?'

For a second I thought I had misheard the question. Or at the very least misunderstood her meaning.

'I know people get hurt in relationships, Mum, but I don't plan on hurting him, no.'

'That's not what I meant, love.' She rubbed at her forehead and then moved, shifting from the armchair to the sofa. She patted the spare seat and so I joined her. 'We still haven't talked about what happened with your father, and now there's a new person around, I really think that we need to.'

I couldn't find the link.

'What happened with Dad was just an accident, Mum.'

'Was it though, Gillian?'

The question hit me with force. She had accepted it all so easily; fabricated our cover story as if she'd had it ready for years. I had never imagined that we would arrive at a place where that was questioned. She had always seemed so safe. I had clearly underestimated her, and shame on me for that.

I considered alterative responses to the query, but I couldn't find anything that felt even remotely appropriate. And it felt much like my mother knew that would be the case.

'Gillian?' she pushed.

I flicked through things as quickly as I could but I couldn't find anything to give her. I hated her for being so neutral. I was panicked, unnerved, and I was sure that my mother should feel much the same. But there was no sign of it. Instead she was the picture of calm, as if this entire conversation had gone to plan; as if I had somehow become so predictable that she knew my moves before I had even thought to make them. The prospect made me hate her all the more.

After nearly thirty seconds of silence I think my mother intervened through pity alone. She pulled in a greedy amount of air before unleashing her words, throwing them out in such a rush that they were run-ons to each other, as if attached by connective tissue.

'I know what you do, Gillian. I know what's in the box upstairs.'

Burn Notice. 2007. Jeffrey Donovan. 'Sometimes the truth hurts. In these situations, I recommend lying.'

'I don't know what you're talking about,' I replied.

Her mouth twitched into an almost-smile. I wondered whether she had expected that response.

'You do know what I'm talking about. You're not stupid enough to not know, love.' There was a compliment in there somewhere, I thought. She sighed and then picked up her speech.

'You thought that I didn't know what you did to the pond when you were younger? You haven't always been as good at covering your tracks as you are now, love, and even now you aren't as careful as you think. When you came home with that box, that look on your face, I knew. I knew that there was something.'

I flicked back to my bedroom and pulled in the memory of bleach, vomit. My mother hadn't had the stomach for what she'd found. Abandoning my denial in favour of honesty was the only clear option that I could see now.

'How did you find out?'

'Things were always dying around you, Gillian. Always.'

And then I had to sit alongside her while she calmly presented her overwhelming evidence for how true this remark actually was. My mother, in a way that mothers are wont to do, could even recall incidents that had long since faded from my own memory store. She discussed my inappropriate enthusiasm when my father, having found a dying fish in the outside pond, had suggested that we freeze it.

'You were so excited,' she said, almost affectionately. 'I should have done something then, really. I do know that.'

Three minutes after the fish, and a sample of the pond water, had been scooped into a sizeable bag and deposited in the freezer, my mother had found me – a small me, perched on the tips of my toes – peering into the top drawer of the freezer, trying to garner a look at the creature. The way my mother told the story, she had shushed me away with a 'You don't want to see that, love' and, defeated, I slid down to sit on the kitchen floor, my knees pulled up to my chest and my back firmly against the freezer unit. I stayed there until my father removed the bag later in the evening. And as I listened to my mother retell this for a second I thought she was right; she really should have done something.

'You know that it's not normal, don't you, Gillian?'

I swallowed a laugh as my mother, of all people, approached the topic of normality.

'At university, we do these things.'

'Things like what's in that box?'

She had me on that one, I'll admit. I couldn't say yes, and I think she knew it.

'I want you to talk to Louise about this.'

'Mum, I can't–'

'It's a not a suggestion, love, it's a stipulation.' Her tone was curt, more serious than I had heard it in years. 'Don't you want to stop doing this? Christ, Gillian, do you even know why you're doing it?'

'Because I like it' didn't feel appropriate. She wanted a concrete explanation, something she could understand. I already knew by then that the experiments were a compulsion. And I knew that I didn't want to stop. I didn't know how I could communicate such thoughts to my mother. The only comfort I could offer her was a half-promise.

'Okay,' I said. 'I'll mention it to Louise.'

I couldn't tell her about it explicitly, that much we both agreed on. Our compromise was that I would discuss my 'anger issues' with Louise, which is what my mother had decided this was – an inappropriate method of dealing with feelings of rage.

'You must have some – how could you not – with your father and all?' she said, creating a causal relationship between his behaviour and my own that I wasn't comfortable acknowledging.

I was – I am – nothing like him. But my mother needed to disassociate herself with this part of my psyche, and I had to allow it, despite the offence caused by her accusation. Anger was a base emotion, and there was a level of complexity here that rage didn't quite fit; I had never hurt anything out of anger, as far as I could recall, but again that hardly seemed like a point worth voicing aloud. I let my mother debase the whole process into something she could understand, something she could pass the buck on – because, I suppose, that's what she needed.

'So we're agreed?' she finished.

Agreed seemed like something of an overstatement but I nodded all the same. An awkward hug followed and I made for my escape. I muttered something about being hungry as I moved to leave the room but my mother pulled me back in.

'Gillian?'

I retraced the three steps I had taken into the hallway and peered back at her.

'You need to get that box out of this house.'

I opened my mouth to dispute this, but before I could find a starting point she concluded: 'It's not a suggestion, love. It's a stipulation.'

Chapter thirteen

My mother had shown a sparkly new aspect of herself that evening, and I felt inclined to conduct myself in a manner that would keep her firmly on my side; having an enemy was difficult but living with one would surely be impossible. After that, I scheduled a follow-up meeting with Louise for two weeks' time; my mother was dismayed by the wait for an appointment but, as I told her, they only had emergency slots free between now and then.

'You don't think this is an emergency?'

'No, Mum, I don't.'

As instructed, I removed the box from our family home. My mother watched me cart the thing out to the back seat of my car, and nothing more was said on the matter. I suppose she assumed I'd disposed of it somewhere, which in a fashion was true; I took them straight to Daniel's house. I told him that they were university experiments and that he was welcome to take a look if he wanted to, but before I could launch into a more comprehensive explanation of the contents, he held his hand up.

'You mean, like, dead animals and stuff?'

'Well, bits of them.'

He swallowed hard.

'I know all I need to know, GT. Just leave the box at the bottom of the stairs.'

Psychology is frequently assessed as a fake science of sorts, but so-called reverse psychology certainly has some merits when employed in real-life situations.

'Won't your aunt mind me leaving them here?' I asked.

I was yet to meet Daniel's aunt, but from what he had said of her already – namely her insistence on meeting me coupled with her incessant questions about the neighbours – she seemed the type of woman who was likely to pry.

'Mind? She won't even know. As soon as you've gone I'm putting those babies in the back bedroom where no one is likely to stumble across them.'

Daniel, as it turned out, was the best excuse for leaving the house with little to no explanation of where I was going or with whom. My mother, in fact, came to assume that whenever I left the house now Daniel would somehow be involved. Even on the evenings when I offered to stay housebound, to make a determined effort at being a present and fully functioning daughter to my mother, she was all too aware that my head was elsewhere.

'You can't stop thinking about him, can you?'

I was midway through a mouthful of dinner and suddenly quite confused. 'Who?'

She arched an eyebrow before lowering her head and tucking a chunk of chicken into her mouth. She chewed over the meat thoroughly before speaking again.

'Gillian, it's okay to be thinking about a man. You know that, don't you? In fact, love, I'd go as far to say that it's actually quite normal.' She seemed disproportionately pleased by the assessment, trying but failing to hide a smirk. 'Why don't you go and see him when we're finished?'

'But what about our evening?'

'Gillian, there will be other evenings.'

And it was that simple. We finished our dinner over more polite and mumbled conversation and then I left, without any vague questions or wild accusations. And this, I thought, was perhaps my first practical reason for keeping Daniel.

***

The moment I stepped outside I was grateful that I had decided to walk rather than drive. The warm emotion plastered around my house that evening had wrinkled and peeled away from me during the forty-five-minute saunter. It was unexpectedly cold out; the type of cold that would prevent too many people from walking around.

At the front of the house, the porch light bounced about inside its plastic shell. Another light in one of the front rooms peered out from behind nearly closed curtains. Directly above this was a room with no curtains at all, and through this uncovered frame I could see a bulb hanging bare. I watched this window for longer than the others, but when a full minute had rolled by I decided that the light had been left on by mistake. He was probably distracted, perhaps tending to her, and I couldn't reason why that thought provoked me so much. I wondered what he could be doing, how he was busying himself, whether he was giving her all of his attention, or whether they spent their evenings in separate rooms. That would explain the amount of lights flickering about the house. Another one appeared then, this one at the side of the building. An upstairs bathroom, perhaps? The light tumbled out through the open window for just under two minutes before it snapped off again. I was convinced I'd heard a toilet flush.

Would he close the window later, when I'd gone?

Was that window always open?

Or was that just a slip? After an unusually difficult day?

When I had seen him earlier there had been something different about him, although I

couldn't work out the specifics at the time. He was usually so focused away from her, devoted to getting through the task at hand, so that he might get back to her. I had seen that determination several times now: during the food shop, once on a walk home, twice while he was out running. I wondered whether it was this sudden difference that had made him forget about the window that he'd opened.

I followed the lights around the house for twenty-three minutes and the same ones remained switched on, the same window still open. What was he doing? Pacing around, or watching television?

Was she pacing around with him – was she even a pacer? I couldn't envisage her trailing about the house after him. Instead I saw her tucked away, in her own little room, where she could stare longingly at the door and wait for him. I imagined him walking in to check on her, and how her whole body would lighten when she saw him; how her head would perk up, how she might shake with happiness. And then, I thought, they'd probably sit and stare through the window together.

It must be beautiful to be so simple.

I checked my watch and made a note of the time; I was a little earlier than usual. In the future it would be better to visit later again, to see whether that top window was still open. Several minutes passed before my mobile phone shook inside my pocket. A new voicemail had arrived. I'd been so engrossed in my viewing that I hadn't even noticed it ring.

'Hi, Gillian, it's me. I'm sorry that I've been a little quiet today. It really has been a funny old night with Emily and – and I definitely didn't call you to moan about that. Ah, I called your house phone but there was no answer there either. Guess you're out or something. So, call me, when you get this? Oh, it's Daniel, by the way. I can't remember whether I said that.'

Nothing appeared to have flickered or altered in the time it had taken to listen to Daniel's message. And it looked like nothing was likely to. I took down one last mental blueprint of the building, to be sure, and then I skimmed through my phone book to Daniel's name. By the time I looked back at the house, what I assumed was the bathroom light had flicked on again. The open window wasn't a mistake, I thought; he wouldn't have forgotten it twice. In perfect synchronicity, Daniel's 'Hello' coincided with the male silhouette appearing in the illuminated patch of glass. I sucked in a stream of air that I couldn't bring myself to expel.

'Hello? Gillian?'

It was a little louder than his previous attempt.

'I'm here, yes. I'm sorry, I was distracted by something.'

'It must have been something good.'

He was fishing.

'Fairly good, yes.'

'Oh, well, ah, I can call you back another time, if I've caught you at a bad time now? Because – wait, no, you called me. Right?'

I half-listened to Daniel tie himself in knots and I half-watched the silhouette as it bobbed in and out of the window frame.

'Sorry, yes, I called you.'

Why had I called him?

Paul disappeared from the frame and snapped the bathroom light off behind him. I could concentrate on Daniel now. I half-listened to his chatter about how modern technology only seemed to work when it suited itself, then I started my pace home, walking with more determination than I could really explain. I had walked as far as Runner's Route when something on the pavement in front of me caught my eye.

'How's Emily?' I asked, filling the empty space in our conversation.

The something was a small bird, covered in fur-like feathers; it was attempting to launch itself, but failing every time. On its third attempt it managed to lift itself several millimetres into the air. I had lifted my own foot three inches off the ground when Daniel started to speak, but then lowered my boot a good two inches clear of the creature. It wouldn't have done much for me, I knew, but there was certainly something tempting in the opportunity.

'Can we not talk about Emily?' Daniel's voice cracked midway through the question and I felt inclined to push for an explanation why; he had, after all, mentioned her himself in his voicemail.

'Has something happened?'

'Things just aren't very good, GT.'

'With her cancer, you mean?'

Daniel breathed heavily into the phone. 'Yes, Gillian, with her cancer,' he said, his tone more curt.

I looked at the bird again, considered Daniel's tone, his anguish, then said: 'Do you mind if I come over to your house?'

Daniel took a beat longer than I expected to answer.

'I really don't want to talk about Emily, Gillian. The whole thing is a mess and she's really unwell at the moment and I just don't know how much sense I'll string together out of all of that. It's just really difficult and she's not even herself at the moment, and it's crazy to try to piece someone else's feelings together, you know?'

I didn't know much about what he was trying to say, but I could see that for something that he didn't want to talk about particularly, he had already found a fair amount to say. Noting my silence, Daniel started again. 'I've not long got back from the hospital either. It's late. I don't want to drag you out at this time of night, really.'

'I'm already out,' I told him. 'You'll be keeping me company.'

I took one last look at the bird before I continued pacing along the pavement. Pulling my coat a little closer around me, I promised Daniel I wouldn't be long before I ended the call.

Chapter fourteen

The front door opened so promptly that I thought Daniel must have been looking out for me. When he stepped out to greet me, I saw that his hair was a little more ruffled than usual, and he looked particularly boyish in his Batman pyjamas. His smile offered great reassurance but as he raised his right arm to rub at the back of his neck, the smile gave way to a nervous laugh.

'Consider me your hero?' he said.

'Do you have tea?'

'Brewing in the kitchen.'

'Then you must be a hero.'

Daniel tried to smile; there was something inauthentic about the expression. He stepped away from the doorway and gestured me inside but, even though I was the person who initiated this visit, there was a moment of hesitation on my part.

'Do you want me to bring your tea outside?'

'No,' I said, forcing a smile.

There was something new here that I was struggling to decipher, but I knew that I couldn't communicate that. I stepped through the front door and hovered as Daniel pushed it shut behind us both; he edged past me and walked along the hallway towards a closed door.

'Come in and we can set the world right.' I didn't respond, and so Daniel added: 'Or we can just sit and drink tea; that's okay as well.'

He pushed open the door to reveal a display of aging worktops and well-worn wooden cupboards. It may even have been the same kitchen that had been here when the house was first built. He pulled out a seat at the table then and wandered into a corner to fill cups and pour milk. The seat looked like it might collapse underneath me but it would have been rude to ignore the gesture. I watched Daniel fish out the tea bags and thump them down on a saucer before carrying the cups to the table. The finished product was such a deep brown that I wondered whether my memory of watching him add milk had been imagined. But there was something dangerous about criticising someone's ability to make tea. I lifted the cup, took a restrained sip, and set it back down on the table.

'Too strong?'

'It's perfect.'

In the less-forgiving light of the kitchen I could see now that there was something wrong with Daniel's face; more specifically his eyes. The skin that surrounded them was pink, irritated, maybe even a little swollen, and I remembered what these three things usually meant.

'Something's upset you?' I asked.

He pursed his lips into a thin line and shook his head. But I spotted his lie this time.

'What were you doing out and about at this hour anyway?' Daniel asked, making it sound much later than it actually was.

'Why don't we talk about Emily?'

'I thought we were going to talk about you?'

I couldn't remember agreeing to that. 'Haven't we got time to talk about you as well?'

He expelled a long stretch of air, sipped his tea, and said nothing.

I could appreciate the heavy burden of upset, and I understood the knock-on effect that was having on his ability to perform adequately in a conversation. However, I lacked the skills required to build an exchange on a foundation of one-word responses, and so I waited until Daniel was ready to say more.

'I'm sorry, GT, I'm not much of a talker at the moment.'

No, I thought, *you aren't.*

Neither of us spoke for some time, but instead sipped our respective cups of tea until we reached the dregs of the drinks.

'Do you feel like talking yet?'

'I'm not sure what there is to say, Gillian.'

'You could say what happened.'

He swallowed so hard that a thudding noise emerged from his throat.

'This is too heavy, GT. We've known each other for five minutes, and this is really not your stuff to deal with.'

'Why not?' I asked.

Daniel tilted his head and smiled at me in a way that felt a little patronising. I couldn't understand what was so heavy, or why sharing the weight was such a terrible idea.

'You're sweet,' he said, which I took to be patronising again.

'I don't mean to be.'

Daniel took a hard look at me and sighed. 'They found another tumour. They can't, or won't – whatever, I don't suppose it makes a difference; either way it's not coming out. They've offered her more treatment, chemo and the rest of it, but it won't cure her. It'll never cure her, they say, it'll just keep her alive a bit longer, and she doesn't want that any more.'

'She doesn't want to be alive?'

He winced again. I thought he might cry but the urge to weep seemed to pass as quickly as it had arrived. While Daniel battled with this new wave of emotion I looked down into my teacup, my hands still tightly clasped around it. It was the only thing I could think of to give him some privacy. I became so absorbed with this that I barely noticed Daniel moving towards me until I felt the inside of his hand rest around the outside of mine. I kept perfectly still, half-scared of making any sudden movements that would either disturb or develop this contact. I was unsure of which I wanted. Daniel gently kneaded his fingertips against my hand before pushing out a deep sigh.

'Okay, I'm done on this for now, GT. Your move.'

He leaned back in his chair, pulling his hand away, and I instantly missed the contact.

'My move?'

'It seems like something is up.'

I didn't realise Daniel was so perceptive.

'It's just my mum,' I started, knowing that I needed to give him something. I had hoped that alone would be enough but when I looked up and found Daniel, wide-eyed and expectant, I saw that he needed more. 'She keeps asking about you, that's all.'

Daniel gave a half-laugh. 'And that's what this trouble is over? She's your ma, she's meant to ask questions.'

'She's nervous, I think.'

'That's understandable too.'

'Why?'

'Because you're her baby?'

Daniel and I were coming at this from very different angles, I had to remind myself.

'No, I mean, I think she's nervous that I'm going to hurt you.'

And just like that, the truth was out.

'Pfft, you must be a real heart-breaker, GT.'

'I don't think I understand.'

Another laugh emerged as Daniel rubbed at the back of his neck. 'Usually parents worry about their own kids getting hurt, especially when it's a girl. No offence, obviously. I mean, usually a parent isn't worried about the other kid getting hurt, so for your mum to be worried about me and not you, that must make you a love 'em and leave 'em kinda girl, do you see?'

Extremely Loud and Incredibly Close. 2011. Jonathan Safran Foer. 'Why couldn't I be the kind of person who stays?'

'I understand, but I don't think that's it, really.'

'No? A girl like you hasn't left a trail of emotional devastation behind her?'

I flinched. A girl like me.

'You're quite lovely to look at, Gillian,' he added, as though he'd noticed my reaction.

'Oh.'

'Which is a good thing,' he offered.

Of all the possible connotations and meanings I could have attached to what Daniel meant by 'a girl like me', my physical make-up wouldn't have even made the top ten. I knew it was a good thing. But it was also a new thing, a slightly uncomfortable thing.

'Thank you,' I said.

'You're welcome.' He moved his hand back around mine. 'So you're not planning on breaking my heart, then?'

'It's not in my summer timetable, no.'

We shared a smile which evolved into a laugh. But after a minute Daniel came back down to earth. His smile drained away and was replaced by something inexplicably pensive.

'Did I say–'

'Sorry, no, you didn't say anything, GT.' He stalled here but the explanation was clearly incomplete. He pulled in a long breath before he continued. 'It feels a bit wrong, sometimes, starting something with you.' I didn't know what expression my own face fell into then but whatever it was, it prompted a quick chorus of apologies from Daniel. 'Christ, I didn't mean that how it came out, at all. I just meant with Emily, and what's happening with Emily. You and I will outlive her, you know? There's something – I don't know, there's something sort of weird about that.'

I'd never thought about it in those terms, but yes, I supposed there was something peculiar about it. But there was also something a little bit exciting.

'Tea?' I thought that we might have had enough tea but Daniel nodded anyway.

I moved from his eyeline to make the beverage that I didn't even want to drink, all for the sake of giving him the space he needed to talk. And this, I thought, was the sort of sacrifice you had to make when you liked someone, feeling pleased with this sudden understanding. While I hovered about the kitchen Daniel talked his way through a spectrum of emotions. He tried so hard to find the right words while overlooking the one that would summarise everything he had just said: Daniel felt guilty. It wasn't a feeling that I had first-hand experience of, but I knew enough of it to recognise the symptoms.

'She knows about you and everything, and she's really happy,' he said as I placed the refilled cup down in front of him.

I smiled, unsure of what I was meant to take from this. 'How can she be happy?'

Although it was likely rhetorical, I couldn't help but put some real thought into this.

'Something has happened, and I know that I shouldn't be telling anyone this, but I really feel like I need to,' Daniel said, changing the tone then.

I felt what I thought must have been empathy. Unknowingly, Daniel had just described my entire life in one sentence. I nodded to indicate that I understood, more than he could know. His hand was tucked around mine when he began talking again, but as he spoke I shifted, quickly wrapping my fingers around his and allowing them to settle there, our extremities comfortably intertwined.

'You can trust me,' I said, and I think we both believed it.

'It's so hard to see someone you love in pain every day and not be able to help them,' he started. 'And up until recently I would have done anything, like, actually anything, to help her. But now, she's asked me to help her to do something, like a dying wish – I don't even know what you'd call it – but it's something I'm not sure about. I mean, I'm not sure I can do it. Instead I just leave her there.' His voice picked up in volume as he raised an outstretched arm and gestured somewhere beyond the kitchen. Towards the hospital, I assumed. 'I leave her there and I tell her to have a good hard think about what she's actually asked me to do, like I'm bloody reprimanding her.'

There was a satisfying twinge in my stomach. Daniel had moved carefully around the issue, I'll admit, but I could take a perverse and reasonably well-educated guess at what had happened. Or more specifically, I could guess at what a dying woman might ask of her carer. I squeezed his hand to pull his attention back to me and watched as his expression slowly softened.

'Daniel, could I meet her?' I asked, more curious than ever about the woman in question.

He smiled and returned my squeeze.

'I think she'd really like that, GT, yeah.'

Chapter fifteen

Emily remained hospital-bound for longer than anticipated after that. An infection had found its way into her system after her most recent stint of exploratory surgery – 'An infection, in a hospital. Christ, what sort of place are they even running?' Daniel had asked, understandably frustrated and irrational – which detained her for several days longer than originally expected. Even following her release she wasn't firing on all cylinders, so Daniel said, but he wanted her to meet me anyway. Neither of us would say so, but I suspected a concern was lingering inside

Daniel by then: if I didn't meet Emily soon, I might not have a chance to meet her at all.

'Only if you're comfortable meeting her, GT. This is a big step, I know.'

'A big step?'

'You know, meeting the family and all.'

'No, it's a great idea for me to meet her,' I said, brushing over the fact that it had been my idea to do so in the first instance.

We entered Emily's bedroom – the would-be dining room of the house – as a team, Daniel holding the door open and stepping in close behind me. The space was an end-of-life sanctuary. Tucked into the corner there sat a bed with a bent mattress, the style that belonged in a hospital, complete with adjustable bars. The rest of the room boasted a mash-up of misplaced furniture. Two feet along from a bedside table there was another table, lower and three-legged, it leaned against the wall for partial support. On top of this there was box upon box, bottle after bottle of medication; beneath it, there was a stack of magazines where the missing leg had once been. I wondered what the magazines were, whether Emily – after breaking the table one afternoon – had bolted to the nearest newsagent and pulled down a pick and mix of publications, long before cancer had confined her to this room. Against the opposite wall there stood a dressing table, complete with a large mirror. The reflection was disturbed by the photographs wedged into the wooden frame around the glass, and I had to swallow the urge to look at them in detail.

There was a large window, shielded by Venetian blinds. They were rolled down but angled open, so that a viewer positioned at the right height would be able to see through. And, sitting in a high-backed armchair by this window, was Emily. Her frame was so petite and the armchair so oversized that I worried the furniture might swallow her. As she shifted higher, no, lower, no, a little higher again to gather a better view of the neighbours, it was impossible not to notice how the invading streaks of sunlight hit her head, which was mostly void of hair bar a few candyfloss wisps.

'Keith Watson's got his granddaughter here again, Danny.'

There was a strength in her voice that I hadn't expected; her tone gave a nod to a northern accent.

'Emily, I've brought Gillian to meet you.'

Daniel shifted into her line of vision and I followed; she tilted her head towards us both. With that first glance from her, I met scrutiny. She eyed me in a way that suggested a surveyor's report of sorts may follow. As she considered me, I noticed a small indent in her right cheek, reminiscent of Daniel's own, as she struggled to pull her mouth into a smile. We held eye contact for a beat too long and I was thankful when Emily pulled her glance away, averting her eyes and shifting her hand towards her mouth to catch a cough that both looked and sounded particularly painful. She leaned forward then and held her uncontaminated hand out towards me. It was skeletal, and I was suddenly quite concerned that my usual handshake might break her fingers.

'Gillian.' She said the name like she was tasting it, and then added: 'Mind if I call you Gillie?'

Under different circumstances, I would have said 'absolutely not'. No one had ever abbreviated my name and it seemed an unnecessary habit to encourage now. But I recalled how Daniel had become Danny, and I wondered whether this abbreviation was Emily's mark of approval.

'Of course, please do.'

The tight smile she wore relaxed a little.

'Marvellous, Gillie. Call me Emily, by the way, given that this oaf hasn't actually introduced us. Danny, you'll have to make us girls some drinks if you expect us to get to know each other.'

Daniel laughed from somewhere behind me. 'Oh, of course, we can't have a guest without having a brew; that just wouldn't do at all. Gillian, do you want to help me in the kitchen?

'You make ten cups of tea a day. What could you possibly need help with?' Emily said, and before Daniel could answer she continued: 'She doesn't want to help, Danny, now scoot.'

Daniel seemed amused rather than offended. He must be accustomed to this, I thought. He flashed raised eyebrows and a half-smile at me as he pulled the door closed, leaving 'us girls' to get to know each other.

'Please, Gillie, take a seat.'

The same frail hand now gestured to a brightly-coloured armchair that sat opposite. It

looked just as overinflated as the one in which she was wedged so I lowered myself down with care, for fear that I was also at risk of being swallowed by enthusiastic cushions. I needn't have bothered. When my buttocks came into contact with the seat it became clear that I had been encouraged to sit on something that, in terms of comfort, resembled a concrete slab.

'I don't usually like my guests to stay too long,' she said, noticing my expression.

A mischievous and throaty laugh followed. I was instantly fond of Emily. Her honesty, alongside these undertones of a calculating nature, was refreshing. In the minutes that followed, she peered through the gaps in the blinds, presumably at neighbours that I couldn't crane my neck far enough to see.

'Anything interesting happening your side?'

'Not that I've noticed, I'm afraid,' I said, not realising that I was meant to be looking.

'Oh, you'll notice all sorts when you're my age. All sorts.'

It occurred to me then that I knew nothing more of Emily beyond her diagnosis of terminal cancer, which had, admittedly, been enough to pique my interest. I needed to ask the woman something. I eyed her left hand and noted the absence of a wedding band, the absence of any evidence to suggest one had ever existed there, and said: 'Are you married, Emily?'

An amused 'Pfft!' fell out of her mouth.

'Oh.'

'Don't be too tender, Gillie, it's not a sore subject. I haven't had the best of luck with men, that's all.' She paused to wipe a small gathering of spittle from the corner of her mouth. 'In my experience, they're a little like dogs. If you don't train them properly in the beginning, they will be running riot by the end. And my men do tend to run a little riot.'

I couldn't fit together the withered physicality of the woman in front of me and the confidence she was voicing. Daniel had told me, warned me, that Emily was quieter than her usual self, and so this had been the last thing I was expecting from a woman in Emily's position.

From the smirk on her face I thought she had perhaps expected me to feel this way.

'I'm dying, Gillie, not dead. There's life in the old girl yet.'

She punctuated the sentence with a wink and in that I could see a much younger woman. A healthier woman. Perhaps even a woman who used to be a bit of a handful.

Daniel kicked his way through the door then with an accompanying rattle from the tea tray. Emily scanned the room, looking first at Daniel, then at me, and then back towards the window. She smirked and I wondered whether she too had the feeling that Daniel had been listening to our chatter.

'Did you go to China, Danny?'

'Only the best for you, Emily, so I went one better than China.'

'Hmm, and where's that, dear?'

'Co-op.'

Daniel winked at me as he set the tray down on the table beneath the mirror. A chorus of clinks arose as he grouped together cups, saucers, and teaspoons.

'No sugar for me today, Danny. Gillie here is sweet enough.'

Daniel looked at me; he appeared impressed. I forced out an awkward laugh to show that I had at least acknowledged the compliment. While Emily persisted in her neighbourhood watch, Daniel carried a half-full cup of tea over to her, and as the saucer beneath the cup changed hands it became clear why it was only half-full. Emily's hands shook with the ferocity of an addict absent of a fix. Daniel made sure to keep his own hands beneath the cup until Emily's had properly adjusted to the weight. They shared a knowing smile and I thought that this must be common practice in their household.

Emily took a sip, released a satisfied sigh, and turned to me. 'Danny makes a good cuppa, don't you think?'

'I was taught by the best.'

'Rubbish. He's got a natural talent when it comes to looking out for me, Gillie, you mark my words.' She paused for another sip of tea. 'Don't you have to be somewhere?' The question was directed at Daniel, who then looked at his watch and conjured something that resembled a clucking sound in his throat.

'What, now?'

'It seems as good a time as any, Danny.'

'Ah, okay, so I have to be somewhere. Errands, food shop, all terribly exciting stuff.'

Emily pulled her eyebrows together and shook her head lightly. 'Danny, you're about to start flapping. Go, do something. Gillie is alright where she is, aren't you?' she asked, turning to address me. I was stunned and pleased in equal measure and so offered a restrained nod in response. 'Perfect. Now, Danny.' She turned to face him again. 'You can leave.'

'Emily, you can't just—'

'Leave.'

Daniel huffed and turned to me. 'Will you be okay here for a bit? I won't be long.'

'Daniel, I'm not going to eat the girl.'

When Daniel finally excused himself, I opened my mouth to speak, but Emily held her hand palm up towards me, halting my sentence. When the front door banged shut, she lowered her hand.

'Now we can really have a talk,' she said, in a way that made her intentions sound more threatening than perhaps intended. 'You can tell me all about you two lovebirds.'

Her use of the term lovebirds left me uncomfortable, although from her overemphasis on the word I thought perhaps she knew it would have that effect.

'We bumped into each other at a restaurant and—'

'Good God, that was you?'

'Yes.'

'I thought Danny had made the whole thing up.' She tagged a small laugh onto the end of her sentence.

'Where did you think he'd been for the evening?'

There came an almost dismissive wave of the hand before she answered. 'Boys will be boys and all that. He could have been anywhere for all I knew. But I certainly didn't believe dinner with a strange girl as his cover story.' She laughed again. 'The excuses my first husband came up with when he was out late – I bumped into so and so; I was out with whoever, from work, yada yada,' she said, waving her hand again. 'I didn't want to guess what Danny might have been doing.'

'You have been married, then?' I asked, sensing the opportunity for a subject change. Emily married her first husband – one of three, as it turned out – on her eighteenth birthday.

'It was all very romanticised, Gillie. I remember feeling like I'd been sold a dud one about two months in, if I'm honest.'

Throughout our time together that afternoon she punctuated her stories with glances through the window and occasional tangents about neighbours I wouldn't recognise, should I ever meet them in person. She provided brief overviews – a highlights reel, she called it – of her marriages and then her career. 'A once-upon-a-time dancer until I got pregnant,' she said with such flippancy that I felt like this pregnancy – and, presumably, the subsequent child – were things I should already know about. I bit down on the urge to ask where this offspring was now, and why Daniel had been the one left to care for Emily.

Emily delivered her stories with a cheerful tone but there was something sad about her face for the duration of our talk. They were fond memories, that much was clear, but perhaps still painful to revisit.

'Do you have any regrets?'

Before Emily could answer her eyes watered; she held back from blinking, presumably for fear of sending the tears tumbling down her face. I wasn't sure what I'd done, but it was clearly a very wrong move. Abandoning my seat, I squatted down in front of her instead and took up her small hand in my own.

'I'm sorry, I didn't mean to pry.'

'Oh,' she half-started, pulling her hand back from me to rub a fingertip under each eye, catching at the tears before they could escape. 'There's no such thing as prying too much, Gillie. It's quite nice to run through the old scrapbook, actually, just stirs up one or two things, you know?' She took a long hard look at me then, as if realising something, but she didn't share her revelation. 'Anyway, another life, that was,' she said, steadying her voice. 'You must be sick of my rambles by now, and that Danny must be on his way home, so give me the last few details. You two seem to be seeing an awful lot of each other.'

Before Emily could steer the conversation down an unwelcome avenue – 'Things must be quite serious with you two, then?' – the front door opened and slammed, and Daniel tumbled into the room laden with carrier bags.

'You needed to go the supermarket, today?' I asked, instantly realising how redundant the question was. 'But it's Tuesday; who does their food shop on a Tuesday?' Paul, I thought, now deeply uncomfortable with the image of him and Daniel in such close proximity.

'So if you're home for the afternoon, then I can unleash Gillie back into the wild, yes?' Emily added.

'Ha, if she'd like to be unleashed, then yes.'

I followed Daniel back into the hallway. He asked if I would call him later and I promised that I would, before shouting another quick goodbye back into Emily.

'Gillie?' she shouted back. With my feet still firmly planted in the hallway I craned my neck around the doorframe to look back in on her. 'Same time next week?' she said, with a wink.

And after that, Tuesday and Thursday afternoons became time ear-marked for Emily.

Chapter sixteen

My mother and I coasted along to my appointment with Louise, alluding to but never directly discussing the so-called anger issues that had led us here. On the morning of the appointment, as I was mentally preparing myself for the lies I was about to tell, my mother offered what I thought was intended to be words of encouragement on the matter.

'You'll be okay.'

I wasn't sure whether it was a question or a command.

'And you know what you're discussing with her this time?' she said, as though I hadn't known what to say for myself during my previous encounter with the woman.

I nodded again, and then offered my mother monosyllabic answers to her semi-concerned questions and mostly redundant advice, ahead of leaving nearly an hour early, now desperate to escape home.

***

On entering the appointment room Louise steered me in the direction of the sofas. We sat opposite each other, in silence, while she fumbled through a collection of notes, the majority of which must have belonged to someone else, I remember thinking, because I surely couldn't have given her that much material from one meeting alone. She looked tired that day, worn down; maybe I was the last hurdle on a particularly difficult Wednesday. Which didn't bode well, given that it was only lunchtime and so she presumably had an onslaught of further issues to contend with from whoever was booked in for her afternoon. She wore black jeans this time, with a white shirt that would have been neat had it been properly ironed beforehand. As it was, it only compounded her worn-out exterior.

'How have you been, Gillian?'

Rather than looking at me while talking she instead maintained eye contact with the pad in front of her, scribbling what I assumed was the time and date in the upper margin while waiting for my reply.

'Okay, mostly. How are you?' I said, half to be polite, and half because she really did look like she needed someone to ask. She pressed her lips together and for a second I thought she may be on the cusp of launching into a genuine answer.

'I'm very well, thank you.'

'You look a little tired.'

'Gillian, that's not really…' She paused, closed her eyes for a beat too long for it to be a blink, and then started again. 'Why don't we just get stuck in for today?'

'Okay.'

'I was a little surprised you called for a follow-up appointment.'

It wasn't a question but she stared at me expectantly, like she'd asked something.

'There are some things that my mother wants me to talk through.'

'So this is another appointment for your mother?'

I hadn't said that, had I?

'No, it's not – well, she's not here, so it's not an appointment for her, no.'

Louise set her notepad down on the seat alongside her. She crossed her right leg over her left, tucking her foot behind her calf somehow. Apparently deciding that this was a comfortable position, she focused on me with some concentration. I didn't know whether I was meant to be talking, or performing, but I was sure that, as conventional conversational exchanges went, it was her turn to say something.

'You seem flustered, Gillian.'

'Only because I don't know what I'm meant to be saying.'

'That's an interesting way of phrasing it,' she said as she leaned over and made a quick note of something on a clean sheet of paper. 'There is no meant or should here, remember? We discussed this last time, Gillian. You need to be open in this space.'

I nodded like I understood, despite my mother having offered conflicting advice not two hours ago just ahead of my leaving the house.

'You just need to tell Louise your feelings.'

'Really, Mum?'

'You must have feelings, Gillian.'

I flinched. Her tone was cutting.

'And don't mention the box.'

'Are you okay, Gillian?' Louise brought me back into the room.

'Of course, sorry.'

She frowned, but didn't push. 'So we briefly discussed your relationship with your mother, and your anger at your parents. Let's unpick some of that further today, shall we?' she asked, although I sensed it was rhetorical.

'I think that would be useful, yes,' I lied. Two months ago no one had even thought that I had feelings of anger, and now it seemed to be all anyone wanted me to discuss.

'Talk me through your feelings, Gillian. If we're unpacking them, show me the box.'

Not that box, I thought, *she doesn't want to know about that box.*

'Okay.' I paused, trying to find a starting point. 'When I get agitated I tend to lash out, I suppose, in a way that my mother doesn't approve of, and I suppose her concern is that this behaviour will worsen if I don't do something to stop it.'

'Okay, and do you think this behaviour will worsen?'

My mind flicked to an image – my father lying misshapen at the bottom of our stairs – so abruptly that even after it had dissipated, it took a few seconds for me to catch up with what I had remembered. *Yes*, I thought, *the behaviour will definitely worsen*. But I couldn't admit that to Louise, or my mother.

'Hard question to answer?' she asked, noting my hesitation. I nodded. 'Okay, I won't ask too many specifics, because if you wanted to tell me then you would have done, yes? But, when you lash out, as you phrased it, do you hurt your mother?'

Something pulled at my insides. 'No, I would never do that.'

'Do you ever hurt yourself?'

When I had cut through – sawn through – the rat's cervical vertebrae, I accidentally cut open my palm. It was only a centimetre in length, an inch or so below the smallest finger on my left hand. But I could remember how disruptive it had been. How I'd tried to carry on the procedure without stopping. How I'd been forced to pause, bandage, and pause again when the gauze became soaked with blood that seemed disproportionate for the small cut that had created it. I occasionally hurt myself collaterally, yes, but Louise probably hadn't meant that.

'No, I don't ever do that either.'

'Okay, so, talk me through this lashing out. Is it physical, verbal?'

'Physical.'

'Do you hit things?'

I wondered whether it was disingenuous to say yes. Probably, I thought, but it was also the closest I could tread to an honest answer.

'Yes, I hit things.'

'Because hitting something makes you feel better?'

'Sometimes.'

'And how often does this happen?'

'There used to be quite a gap between them, but then things changed when I went to university.' I remembered the weekly experiments performed for an audience, the excitement at being watched. 'And things have changed again since my father passed away. Things have been different; more difficult, maybe.'

More difficult since Dad? Had I really said that?

I reassessed the sentence as Louise started on another sheet of paper. I had provided her with too much material in such a short space of time.

'Can I be honest?' I threw out, without fully considering what would follow. There was an uncomfortable flutter of something sitting in my stomach that told me I needed to say something.

Louise smiled and, without even finishing the sentence that she was midway through scribbling down the side margin of her page, she set the pad and pen down on the sofa again. Leaning back into the cushions behind her, she flashed her hands, palm up, at me, in a 'the-floor-is-yours' gesture.

'I think my mother's concern is mostly founded on her worry that I'm an angry person, and I think she worries that I'm like that because that's how my father was.' I thought of the box again. Much as I would have liked to blame my father, I had, in fact, brought this whole thing on myself. 'Anger was always an immediate emotion in our house, and my mother seems to think that's been more damaging to me than it actually was. Everyone has something, don't they?'

Louise bunched her eyebrows together. 'What do you mean by that, Gillian?'

'Whatever it is that makes other people do things that they shouldn't. People smoke, and drink, and shop until their credit card is within an inch of its expiry date. But no one rushes them into therapy for it.' I paused and considered what I'd said. 'Sometimes people rush them into therapy for it, in very extreme circumstances.' Was this an extreme circumstance?

'So you're comparing you lashing out, as you phrase it, to these other habits?'

'Yes,' I said, relieved that Louise had managed to decipher my meaning.

'So it's a coping mechanism?'

I stalled again. It was the second time in two sessions that I had lost my way like this; I was concerned that Louise might take it personally now. Although perhaps she should, given that it was largely her fault. This level of acceptance was alien to me. Of all the names she could have given it, she gave it the one that I had been using to validate it for years. Was I cured, then? Was everything about me now much more normal than I had given it credit for being?

'There's nothing wrong with it being a coping mechanism, Gillian. We don't even have to give it that name, if you'd prefer not to.'

It wasn't the name; it was the acceptance. The normalisation of it to someone who was originally intended – in my mother's dreams, at least – to eradicate the issue.

'No, coping mechanism is fine, I think.'

'Everyone has them, as you clearly already know. It's difficult without knowing the specifics of the behaviour, but you'll tell me that when you're ready, I'm sure. There are other things to consider with these things, these coping mechanisms – aside from the concerns it may raise for your mother, which is problematic, I know. The thing you always need to ask yourself is: who is this behaviour actually hurting? If it's hurting no one but helping you, then that in itself is cause enough to allow yourself these' – she fumbled over her phrasing – 'things, these moments.'

And there was that benchmark again.

'One thing that I would say is that there are options for this, and by that I mean there are better – no, sorry, not better necessarily, just different – coping mechanisms available to you. There are ways to lash out, as it were, in a less destructive way, if the destruction of things is the real issue here, and if that's something you'd like to talk through with me in the future.'

'Constructive instead of destructive, you mean?'

She nodded. 'Maybe before the next session, you can think of some ways you might do that?'

I flicked to an image of Daniel. 'Absolutely. I can manage that.'

Louise launched into her stock explanation of how well I'd done. I can't say for certain that it was verbatim to what she had said previously, but the farewells were certainly close. Despite the uncomfortable silences, the hour had moved relatively quickly and while that had minimised the anguish of having to attend this meeting at all, I couldn't stifle a growing worry that something had slipped out that shouldn't have done. I hadn't mentioned the box, and at the time that seemed the most important detail to hold on to.

'If you head back down towards reception then Rachel can sort you out for another appointment. I know you had a little wait for this one, so best to get a jump on for the next one. But you can, of course, call me in the meantime if there's anything you need.'

I thanked her, waited for the door to close shut behind me, and then set off walking in the opposite direction of the reception area.

Chapter seventeen

It was two hours later when I arrived back at home. My mother would have expected me much earlier, I knew. But after the food shop and the thirty minutes spent following Paul – his 'German Shepherd on Board' badge dangling with pride in the back window of his car – the afternoon had largely slipped away from me. And I hadn't even been able to work out where he was going – beyond somewhere that broke his usual routine.

It irked me to be so out of his loop. I tried to shake the feeling away as I emptied my backseat of perishable goods. I had only made it halfway up the drive, heavily laden with bags, when I noticed that my mother was in the doorway. Her feet were twelve inches apart and her hands were on her hips. I heaved myself onto the front doorstep and set the bags down either side of me; their contents had already started to spill out over the floor.

'Your appointment was this morning.'

It wasn't a question, but she clearly expected an answer.

'I've been food shopping. I must have just lost track of time. I thought we could talk through this morning over dinner.'

My mother eyed the shopping with suspicion. What exactly did she think I was trying to smuggle in?

'But you did see Louise this morning?'

The suspicion seemed disproportionate given my impeccable behaviour of late. It felt unwarranted and, as such, I felt offended.

I was suddenly quite aware of a slump in my shoulders, a downwards pull at the corner of my mouth. I hoped that I had created a look of disappointment, but would have settled for bemusement. Without saying a word I squatted down to the bags around my feet and gathered their handles. I stood slowly, in order to distribute the new weight around me.

'Look, Gillian, I know that you think–'

'Some of this needs to be chilled or it will be useless. Excuse me.'

She allowed enough room for me to waddle through the doorway and into the house. Two food-stuffed bags hit her shin and I decided it wasn't worth an apology. Instead I quietly continued on my way to the kitchen. I counted through the first minute when the kitchen door swung open, as if my mother were counting as well. I busied myself by setting the oven temperature, organising the vegetables, stashing the apple pie – which had definitely been my mother's favourite thing at some point – in the fridge, shortly followed by a canister of whipped cream. She could stand and watch me for as long as she wanted to. I would not speak first. The water was boiling for gravy and I was dicing an onion when my mother gathered together the nerves to say: 'I'm sorry if I've upset you, Gillian.' She crossed the room as she spoke, and then took a seat at the small dining table behind me.

'I'm not upset,' I said. But I thought I was allowed to be.

'I was just thinking all sorts of nonsense when you didn't come home from that appointment. I know you were nervous, must have been nervous, talking to her about that sort of thing and it just got me thinking that–'

'It's clear what you were thinking.'

I added boiling water to the gravy granules and stirred until the mixture was smooth, then I threw in the diced onion. The mixture sat cooling on the work surface while I rummaged through the freezer to pick out the bag of chicken that I had only minutes ago shoved in. My mother continued to reflect. Her elbows were propped on the table, her hands cradling her chin, and her eyes had narrowed on a random spot on the floor.

'Gillian, I appreciate that you're an adult,' she started. 'But you need to appreciate one or two things as well. This hasn't been easy, you know, finding that box and accepting that behaviour from you.'

When I turned to face her I was already wearing a frown that I couldn't shift.

'But if we're going to go down this therapy route, which I really think we should because I'm not at all fond of the alternative, then I just need to know, and trust, that you can be honest with me. And it works both ways, love, because you need to trust that you can confide in me without me overreacting, or, I don't know, you just need to trust me with these things.' She paused here and gave a shallow sigh, almost a huff.

Before I Go To Sleep. 2014. Nicole Kidman. 'Don't trust anyone.'

My mother continued: 'Trust that you can tell me things without me doing whatever it is you're nervous of me doing.'

What, like making me go to therapy? I wanted to push, but instead I nodded to indicate that I had heard her; I stood silently, arms folded, as I processed her speech. Not at all fond of the alternative, she had said. Which was what? I wanted to ask but swallowed the question.

'Is there anything you haven't told me, that you feel like you should tell me?' she pressed.

The situation hadn't developed as I had planned. The unpredictability of my mother these days made it more challenging to anticipate her reactions to certain stimuli. I had assumed that this would lead to something much more explosive; that the calm attitude would finally give way to something much more interesting, and it would then fall to me, the considerate daughter, to defuse the situation with a touching display of emotion. But my mother had beaten me to it. And worse still, she had upped the ante. This would take something exceptional.

I walked over to her side of the table and, standing next to her, I held my arms outstretched towards her. My mother stood and complied. It was a good and convincing hug, I felt sure of it. The next stage in my plan proved more taxing.

'I love you, Mum.'

The words rushed out, one on top of the other. A hand came up to pat the back of my head then. We stayed close like that for a handful of seconds before my mother pulled away and I went back to cooking. I didn't say anything at all about the fact that she hadn't said it back.

'Do you want to tell me about this morning, love?'

'There isn't much to tell, really. She gave me some good ideas.'

'Ideas for what?'

My mother was hoping for an epiphany. I left the knife suspended but loosened my grip around it slightly as I considered my explanation. I threw out an overview of the morning's events, delivering to my mother small pebbles of information that I thought would appease her, including the plan to deal with my so-called anger in constructive rather than destructive ways, which she hmm'd over. When she changed the subject to something more palatable, I knew that my retelling had pacified her.

'And have you spoken to Daniel today?'

'Earlier, yes.'

'Is he well?'

I couldn't remember whether I had even asked him.

'A little stressed,' I said, thinking that this was likely the truth. 'He has some family troubles at the moment.'

'I wouldn't want to rush you, because I know what a big thing meeting the family is and all,' she said. It seemed that everyone, apart from me, could appreciate the magnitude of introducing someone new to the family. 'But it would be nice to meet this boy, you know?'

'Why don't I invite him over for dinner?'

The question popped out, bold and fully formed. The determined silence that followed indicated that my mother had been surprised by the suggestion too. Some time rolled by before she managed to say anything at all, and I found myself so preoccupied with thoughts of Daniel – and the warm feeling in my abdomen that was a standard response to him now – that I almost missed her reply.

'That's a lovely idea, but not tonight.'

'No, no, not tonight. But, soon?'

***

Three days later, after spending the afternoon with Emily, I slipped the suggestion of a family dinner into my goodbyes with Daniel. His usual composure abandoned him and gave way to a sudden wave of what appeared to be panic.

'I'll have to check with Emily. I try not to leave her often,' he said.

It took another four visits but we eventually decided on a convenient date for everyone.

'What time do you want me?'

'Half past six?'

Four hours later the front doorbell interrupted my mother's unwelcome critique of my outfit for the evening. Behind the door there stood Daniel, wearing his lopsided smile and his corduroy jacket that I had grown quite fond of. In his right hand he held a bottle of wine which, as I glanced down towards it, he promptly lifted until it was level with my chest. He held the bottle securely at arm's length as if there were something dangerous about it. I reciprocated his smile, and his nervousness, and took the bottle from him.

'I've never seen you drink wine,' he said.

'No, but it's polite that you brought it.'

He laughed and rubbed at the back of his neck. 'Emily's orders.'

I stepped aside and gestured him into the house. My mother was hovering behind me, her eyes wide and expectant. She took an enthusiastic step towards us and, in my peripheral vision, I was sure that I saw Daniel flinch.

'Mum, Daniel. Daniel, this is Geraldine.'

I knew this introduction was right. I had seen it so many times.

My mother ushered us towards the dining room before I could say anything interesting about either of them. When we walked through the open double doors it was clear that she had gone to some effort in making the room look presentable. To her credit, it did look very well put together, although not as appealing as it had done when there had only been two place settings.

'Do you know, Daniel, this is the first special occasion we've had for using this table since we moved here?'

There was a satisfied smile on her face as she walked through to the kitchen. Daniel and

I swapped understated smirks of amusement. There was something satisfying about the fact that we now shared a secret.

'I'm sorry. She's a little...' I hesitated.

'Enthusiastic?' Daniel offered.

We had time to share a laugh before my mother burst into the room holding a plate in each hand, with a third one precariously balanced on her left forearm. She distributed our meals before sitting down with her own, at which point an awkward silence fell over the table. The three of us exchanged glances as we fought to chew through the circles of mush that sat on our respective plates.

'How are the fishcakes, kids?'

So that's what they were meant to be.

'Certainly the best homemade fishcakes I've ever had, Mrs Thompson.'

It was a physiological battle to stop myself from smirking over Daniel's response. I thought these must be the only homemade fishcakes he had ever eaten, making them the best by default. Regardless of whether there was any truth to Daniel's sentiment, it had been complimentary enough to lure my mother from her shell and, from that point onwards, their only moments of silence seemed to occur alternately while the other one was speaking. My mother quizzed Daniel like he was the first real live human being she had ever encountered. Although, over the course of our mediocre starter, I began to think he might have taken my mother too seriously when she had demanded that he tell her everything about himself. Throughout our main course of roast pork with an assortment of vegetables I continued to learn various things about both of them that I had been ignorant of before. I'd had no idea that my mother used to be a valued assistant at Clive and Jenkins' Accountancy Ltd nor did I know that Daniel was severely allergic to penicillin, something that he discovered right in the middle of a family holiday, much to his mother's annoyance.

Should I have known? Were these normal things to ask?

It wasn't until Daniel was mopping up the remnants of pork-tinged gravy with a round of bread that I became relevant to the evening at all.

'I've really taken you up to when I moved in with Emily now, and when I met Gillian,' said Daniel, punctuating his life story with a curt laugh and a mouthful of food.

When I looked up from my dinner plate, they were both looking back at me.

'That's quite a potted history of Daniel you've been given there, Mum.'

'It really is.' She paused to laugh although I couldn't see why, and Daniel reciprocated the effort. I managed a smile.

'Sorry, I might have missed something here, but who is Emily?' my mother probed
further.

'Oh, she's my aunt. I moved here to care for her. It was a big decision, but you do these things for family, don't you?'

My mother looked inexplicably outraged.

'I told you about Daniel's aunt, Mum.' Because why wouldn't I have told her?

'I'm sure you didn't, Gillian.' She looked back to Daniel. 'You said you care for her?'

'I do. The only other option was a hospice and it just didn't seem right, so, here I am. Nurse Daniel.'

Daniel smiled. I batted the expression back to him in return but my mother's effort at joining in with this display was unconvincing. I was all too aware that I had missed something crucial and whatever it was had made for a sour turning point in the evening.

'Gillian, take Daniel's plate for him and help me in the kitchen.'

She disappeared through the door as she finished speaking. I collected my plate, and Daniel's, and followed her. Behind the kitchen door I found her with her back towards me, her hands hanging on the kitchen work surface, as if attempting to steady herself. Without turning to face me she said: 'Why didn't you tell about his aunt?'

'I find it hard to believe that I didn't, Mum.'

She turned to face me then, leaning back against the work surface. 'Is she going to die, Gillian?'

'I'm not sure that's an acceptable question to ask.'

'Well I'm asking it. Is she?'

At some point in the last minute or so my mother's face had reddened. It looked like she was close to tears and, while I could empathise with Daniel's situation, I couldn't help but think my mother might be taking her reaction too far.

'Yes, she is.'

She closed her eyes. Her right hand came up to her head and she rubbed at her temples. 'Is this why you're involved with this boy?'

'I'm sorry?'

'Gillian, you have nothing, and I mean nothing, in common with him. He is kind, he is the first boy you have brought home, and, well – what am I meant to think?'

I wasn't sure what she was meant to think, but I was sure it shouldn't be what she was apparently thinking.

'We were having a nice normal evening until now, Mum. But now Daniel is sat out there' – I paused to gesture beyond the kitchen in case my mother had forgotten the close proximity of our guest; it was a genuine concern to me what Daniel might have heard, or might hear in the minutes to follow – 'wondering, much like I am, what on earth is going on. I care about him, deeply, I'll have you know.'

The words emerged with a power and conviction that was surprising even to me and I realised then how authentic the sentiment behind them must have actually been. And then something snapped. Some censorship, or sense of parental respect, something that would have ordinarily have held me in my place suddenly sprang open, unleashing: 'How dare you, Mum? I keep a dying woman company and you twist it into this? What the fuck is wrong with you?'

I rushed out of the kitchen, uninterested in any response she might offer. In the next room Daniel was staring at the dining table with disproportionate concentration. He flashed a sad smile when he saw me in the doorway. When my mother joined us seconds later, Daniel thanked her for a pleasant evening but said he really must be getting home.

'I didn't realise the time,' he added, with an awkward laugh.

Like respectable and fully functioning adults, we all said our overtly polite thank yous and goodbyes. When the front door closed I stormed up to my bedroom and stayed there for the remainder of the evening. My mother tried, once, for verbal contact through my closed bedroom door – 'We have to talk, Gillian' – but I had nothing I felt I could say.

Chapter eighteen

Following the argument with my mother I spent more and more time at Daniel's house – or at least, that was the impression my mother was under. She and I exchanged clumsy niceties before I slipped out of the house for a therapy appointment that I hadn't booked, or I left to spend an afternoon with Emily – the latter more often than not was actually true. Emily and I became close friends – dare I use the term – but she never mentioned whatever it was that she'd asked Daniel to do for her (I had my ideas on the matter, all the same). She mentioned a host of other things. We discussed the dancing career – less a career, more something she did to irk her then husband – the child, the near-child that never quite came to fruition, and the divorces. 'There are always divorces, Gillie,' she said, and I nodded like I agreed with her. We even discussed Daniel's parents once or twice. 'It's hard to believe he came from the same stock as them; it's hard to believe that I did,' she'd said, and from what I now knew of their dispassion towards human suffering and their lack of family loyalty, I was inclined to agree.

Late one evening, when Emily had finally settled, Daniel and I were hidden away in the kitchen. We were sitting across the table from each other, hands clasped and mouths silent. I approached the one subject Emily had avoided.

'Did you find a resolution to whatever it was Emily asked you about?'

'What she'd asked me about?'

'She asked you to do something, didn't she?'

Daniel swallowed hard as he registered what I was referring to. 'Ah, yeah, I'm not sure that's something we'll come to an agreement on, GT.' His fingers switched position around mine and Daniel watched them with unnecessary intensity, grateful, I thought, for something to focus on. 'People disagree on things all the time, don't they?'

On another Tuesday morning, some weeks into our scheduled visits, I turned up earlier than Daniel had been expecting me, ahead of him going out for general supplies. In the hallway I eyed my watch – 9:15am – and thought how tardy it was of him to still be bed-shaped when he actually had things to be doing.

'What time do you have to go out?' I asked.

'Pfft, no time, really. I have to shower first. I'm not sure the world is quite ready for this.' He gestured from his dishevelled hair all the way down to the small turtle heads that made up the pattern on his pyjama bottoms. I wondered then what it would be like to sleep next to Daniel, whether I'd sleep at all given the brightness of his attire. He noticed my stare. 'It's not that bad, is it?'

I shook my head. He leaned forward and planted a damp kiss on my forehead, and this time I felt no urge at all to pull away.

'You might want to give Emily a bit of time to come round today. We had a rough night.'

The tardiness made sense now.

I hid myself away in the kitchen and nursed a cup of tea while Daniel showered. The house was so quiet. As if by accident then, I wondered whether Paul's house would be this quiet in the morning, or whether the place would host an ongoing series of clicks as paws paced over wooden flooring. I had seen Paul's hallway only once and from my somewhat shoddy viewpoint at the time it had been hard to gather whether it was carpet, or a carpet rug, sitting at the entrance ahead of a wooden floor. But I had mostly decided on laminate flooring; Paul somehow seemed the type.

Thirty minutes later Daniel returned to the room looking much more presentable. The lemon scent of his shower gel was so pungent that I imagined the whole room felt revitalised just from him having walked into it.

'Well, how do I look?'

His hair was flamboyant, his trousers properly ironed, and the front of his T-shirt was completely devoid of anything resembling a cartoon character. I wondered what the special occasion was.

'Where are you going, looking so neat?'

It was uncharacteristic of me to pry but there was something different – more attractive, even – about Daniel that morning, and an unfamiliar voice in the back of my head was frantically trying to work out why. General supplies, he'd said. What did that even mean?

'Neat?' he questioned.

It was the wrong word but I had to stick with it.

'Yes, neat.'

'Is neat a good thing?'

'Usually. I suppose it depends on where you're going, really. But I don't suppose anyone would ever want to be messy.'

Daniel let out something between a laugh and a 'Hmm' before planting a kiss on my cheek. These little displays had become more commonplace over recent weeks and I was always surprised – and proud, I'll admit – when I succumbed to them this easily.

'You're a peculiar little jelly bean, GT, you really are.'

These little names were commonplace too, although I was less comfortable with them.

'So what should I do with Emily, just go in and sit with her?'

Daniel fidgeted, rubbed at the back of his neck, averted his eyes. I couldn't make the movements fit together meaningfully.

'I'd leave her, if I were you,' he said, staring out of the kitchen window. 'Yep, definitely best to leave her.' With a quick shake of his head, as if shooing away his thoughts, he was back in the room with me. I wondered how bad Emily's bad night had been, and how hard Daniel must be trying to process it. 'I promise that I'll be back soon.'

Daniel excused himself before I had ample time to voice my touching display of genuine concern. I found him in the hallway tugging on a coat.

'Did you say where you were going?' I asked again, all too aware that I was pushing but far too curious of his answer to stop myself.

'So curious today, GT,' he said, evidently holding back a laugh. 'I won't be long.'

And he was gone.

I explored the house – something that I'd done several times already at this stage, but I always managed to find something new – and found myself enamoured by the twenty-one photographs that were dotted around the living room. They were scattered over the tables, the fireplace, tacked onto the wall to make a jigsaw-like feature of themselves – and they watched you every time you moved. I had seen them on earlier visits but had never studied them, not properly, not carefully enough to track one set of physical markers to another. Despite my best efforts, I couldn't match their faces. I couldn't even find Emily.

By the time Daniel had been gone for a little over an hour, I had grown frustrated by the photographs around me. I hadn't managed to tie any two individuals together and it perturbed me, disproportionately so, in fact. I walked from the living room out into the hallway, hoping that there may be signs of life from Emily by now. At home I was always glad of the quiet and solitude but when I was at Daniel's, there was an instant and desperate need for human interaction. I pressed my ear against Emily's bedroom door, and held my breath firmly inside my lungs while scrutinising any sounds hidden by the wood. There was an understated hum from one machine or another but beyond that, there was nothing to suggest it was a good time for me to intrude.

From somewhere inside the kitchen an alarm started to ring; 12:30pm meant that it was time for one lot of medication or another. Inside I found the noise emanating from a small clock balanced on top of a box of what I remembered were painkillers. Emily's medication had slowly increased over recent weeks and, while various nurses tended to her every whim for their allotted time with her, some responsibilities – more responsibilities –

tumbled onto Daniel. 'There are so many, GT. I just can't – I can't chance it, you know?' He had been frantic when he made this argument, despite my having told him that the alarms were a good idea. I put the clock to sleep, setting it to wake up again in another six hours, before washing my hands thoroughly and unloading three white caplets onto a small saucer. 'We need to keep things as clean as possible,' Daniel had said, again frantically, although it had seemed like a perfectly sensible request to me. The first time that I had done this for Daniel – or rather, for Emily – I had only shaken loose one tablet. Now, eyeing the three that had spilled out onto the plate as I took a glass down from the top cupboard, I thought what a testament those tablets were to the worsening state of affairs.

Knock on Any Door. 1949. Nick Romano. No, wait. John Derek. 'Live fast, die young, leave a good-looking corpse.'

'Danny won't even recognise what they put in the ground,' Emily had said two, maybe three, visits ago. I hadn't told Daniel. I never told him when we had conversations like that.

I loaded the saucer and a glass of water onto a tray before dropping four chocolate digestive biscuits onto another small saucer. Daniel rationed these treats now. Despite the utter absurdity of it, he seemed to have convinced himself that a healthy diet might go some way towards counteracting the effects of a fast-advancing stage four cancer. Emily had batted her hand at Daniel's naivety – or was it optimism? 'Let him have it, if it makes him feel like he's doing something,' she had said, and I had been sneaking her the biscuits since. The sudden influx of memories conjured a tug of affection as I pushed through the kitchen door and wandered out into the hall.

With the tray precariously balanced on one hand I pushed down the door handle, eased open Emily's door, and waited for a greeting. It seemed far-fetched to expect a 'Good morning, Gillie', but I had expected something, a rustle of the bedclothes if nothing else. There was a mound of blankets on the hospital-issued bed, beneath which, I assumed, was a sleeping Emily. It seemed almost cruel to wake her but missing a batch of medication could upset her system for an entire day, as Daniel insisted on reminding me on a sometimes hourly basis now. I hoped that there would be something – heavy breathing, some signs of discomfort – that would justify my waking her but there was nothing to suggest that she was anything but peaceful at that moment.

If I make enough noise, I remember thinking, *she'll wake up on her own.* I was disproportionately desperate to escape the guilt of disturbing her. I set the tray down with a deliberate bump on the dressing table and forced out an embarrassingly chirpy 'I think you're due some tablets, Emily.' I made my way closer to the bed, glass of water in one hand and a saucer of pain relief in the other, and although I was walking towards her, it wasn't until I was a mere three steps away that I saw it. The relaxed expression, the unblinking eyes, the tinge of blue that was already chasing its way around the edge of her lips. In an accidentally dramatic gesture I dropped both the glass and the plate and then, without fully considering why, I reached forward to touch her. I ran the back of my hand against her cheek, tucked my fingers firmly around hers, fighting against the onset of rigidity. It was the most peaceful that I had ever see her. And I couldn't have felt more disappointed.

Chapter nineteen

Under normal circumstances I had a reliable method of emotionally dealing with life incidents. It wasn't that I didn't experience emotions, you understand, more that I couldn't – still can't – decipher them adequately and, because of that, my verbal and physical responses to certain stimuli leaves something to be desired. I flicked through my reference bank but struggled to find what felt like an appropriate media representation of someone reacting to the death of a person they weren't biologically related to. Sadness seemed to be the general theme, but I needed something more specific. And something told me that my fail-safe plan of calling my mother for advice wouldn't be appropriate this time.

American Psycho. 2000. Christian Bale. 'I have to return to some videotapes.'

I called Daniel three times, only to be immediately bounced to his voicemail as though his mobile was turned off or lifeless. On the fourth attempt I heard ringing, but I still didn't get an answer. In the hallway I searched through the drawers of a waist-high unit, on top of which sat the house phone. I hoped to find a letter, a name, a phone number, but instead found dozens of letters, about scans, appointments, and every second, third, and fourth opinion available on the severity of Emily's condition. All I found was overwhelming evidence of how hard Daniel had fought to keep her alive, and I felt a sudden pull on my insides then at realising I would have to be the person to tell him that he'd failed in that endeavour.

Unable to find any remotely useful paperwork on how to proceed, I had no other option but to call the police, or an ambulance; I wasn't sure. In my best mock tones of anxiety and panic, I communicated that confusion to the woman on the other end of the phone who asked what my emergency was.

The paramedics came, saw, and confirmed it, on the off chance that I had been stupid enough to miss a pulse or mistake the beginnings of rigor mortis for something else. It looked like it had all happened at some point in the last four hours. Her levels of Adenosine Triphosphate had long since drained from her face and, I suspected, many of her larger muscles were likely affected by now as well. The paramedics didn't explain this to me – 'It looks like she's been gone a little while, pet' was their preferred delivery – but God, how I wanted them to explain it. They talked me through what happened next, who I needed to call, and what I could do until then.

'I'm not the next of kin,' I rushed out, thinking this was something they should know – like it would influence Emily's current state.

From the mass amounts of paperwork that I had managed to wade through, I eventually found a name and a doctor's surgery. The female paramedic offered to call for me, while her male counterpart repeatedly offered his sympathies before asking exactly who I was – a question that should have occurred to him sooner, I thought.

'The doctor is coming out now, pet.'

The doctor, fortunately, knew me as Daniel's friend, so at least she could verify my involvement with the family – sorry, with the deceased. While the medical professionals held their conference together in Emily's room, I paced the hallway with my phone pressed to my ear and my thumb punching the green call button and red cancel button alternately, every time Daniel's answer machine informed me that the person I was calling wasn't available to take my call at the moment. I shut out the chatter and listened carefully, just in case Daniel's forgotten mobile was buried about the house somewhere.

'Come on, Daniel, answer the bloody phone.'

'Miss Thompson?'

'Yes? Sorry, I'm trying to get hold of Daniel.'

'We need you to, really. We can't proceed any further without him.'

When the doorbell sounded – three times in rapid succession – I knew that it was him. He never took his house keys now, not when I was with Emily. He would ring the bell, steal a kiss, and Emily would be none the wiser. Behind the door now he was panting, sweating, and although I was half-prepared to break the news to him myself – in what I hoped would be a soft and appropriate tone – the ambulance that was blocking his driveway had been the only announcement that he needed.

'It's happened, hasn't it?'

***

In the days that followed Daniel wasn't himself. But I suppose that was to be expected. Real people aren't themselves, necessarily, when they're grieving. There were flashes of his normal character but they were quickly undercut by fidgets and awkward stretches of silence. Nevertheless, I went to his house every day without fail. I never thought to ask whether he wanted me there or not, but I do remember thinking: *where else would I be?*

'How are you?'

'Chipper, with a cold front of melancholy sweeping in from the west. Which I think is probably normal.' He stepped away from the doorway and gestured me inside. 'I'm not convinced it's all properly gone in yet, but sorting out the funeral stuff helps, I suppose.'

I followed him into the kitchen.

'Emily had a folder of funeral things,' Daniel explained.

'Plans, you mean?'

'I always told her that she was morbid for doing something like that, and that…' Daniel was facing away from me as he spoke but the crack of emotion in his voice was as unmistakable as the beginnings of tears. 'But maybe she knew that this would happen.

Maybe she knew that when the time came I really would be this fucking useless.'

I stood behind him and wrapped my arms around his body until my hands came to a halt on his stomach. I don't know where the gesture came from, but Daniel seemed pacified by it, a deep sigh escaping him as my hands settled. My chin sat level with where I estimated his first thoracic vertebrae to be, such was our height difference. I breathed in his stale smell – a T-shirt that hadn't dried properly – and on my exhale, I pressed my sympathies into him.

'I'm so sorry this has happened to you, Daniel.'

'Don't be sorry, Gillian; you're not what killed her.'

Daniel didn't ask whether I wanted a hot beverage but he served me a small mug of hot chocolate anyway. I deliberately sat down on the seat next to him rather than opposite. He propped an elbow on the table and balanced his forehead in the palm of his hand as he stared into the drink.

'You just need to give him some time,' my mother had told me, noting the frustration in my tone earlier that day when I had told her that Daniel was fine – too quiet, but fine. 'That's normal, Gillian,' she said. But his quiet was too much for me.

'Is there anything that I can do?' I pushed.

Daniel sighed so hard that his frame drooped. 'I think you're already doing everything that you can, GT.'

I put my arms somewhere around his shoulders and torso then, and pulled him towards me. My fingers hovered at the edges of his hair until his shoulders sagged against me, and the by-products of his sobs were quickly seeping through my T-shirt. It was the first time I thought I may actually be of some use to Daniel.

'I'm just so angry at her, Gillian,' he said, the words muffled against my shoulder. When he pulled away from me, I could see the skin beneath his eyes was red, swollen, glossy from tears that hadn't made it either down his cheeks or onto my clothing. He looked lost. The longer I watched him, the more pronounced my own feelings became. Sympathy, rage, and something that felt much softer battled it out for space in my stomach.

'Why are you angry at her?'

Daniel rolled his eyes as if I should already know the answer. 'Weren't you angry, when your dad died?'

Yes, I thought, *but probably for a different reason.*

I reached out to him and gave his right thigh a small squeeze. I hoped he might find something comforting in the gesture. He inhaled deeply and pushed the air back out in an elongated stream, trying to steady himself.

'This is what she wanted, right?'

He looked across at me for an answer. I nodded.

'She asked me to do this, more times than I can even – Christ, this is absolutely what she wanted. And I understand that, deep down. I understand she wanted things on her terms and she wanted – control? I guess, maybe. This is what she wanted.' He repeated the phrase like an affirmation, reminding himself that Emily was ready for this, until he changed his beat: 'She gave no thought to me, GT. No fucking thought at all.'

'What do you mean?' I pushed again. I knew it, in my gut, but I needed to hear him say it. I wondered how beautiful the words would sound in Daniel's voice.

'I mean she begged me to help her finish things and she gave no thought to what happened afterwards, no thought to me, no thought to how I'm meant to live with this.' Daniel's speech was staggered with caught breaths and unfulfilled sobs as he tried to communicate, and so it took me a moment or two to decipher the words. This was it: Daniel was in an obvious state of emotional turmoil but I couldn't reach him; I was on the opposite end of the spectrum somewhere, with winged creatures occupying my lower abdomen desperate for the big reveal that I now knew was coming.

'I killed her, Gillian. She asked me to help. I did, and now I fucking hate myself for it.' His eyes were clenched shut as the words fell from him, as though he were bracing himself for an inflamed or hurtful response. I tried to beat down a swell of curiosity and excitement but there was only one question I could settle on long enough to ask out loud.

'What happened?'

And he told me. Going back to their first conversation about it, Daniel revisited Emily's most recent hospital stay and sifted through the doctor's report on how the cancer was advancing. 'We can treat you, but I'm afraid it will only be an exercise in lengthening your life at this stage,' the doctor had told them both.

'And what use is that, really?' Daniel interjected into his own narrative. It had been a lot of use at the time, I wanted to remind him, flashing back to when he had scorned Emily's refusal for treatment, but I didn't for fear of disturbing his sequence. She had asked calmly, Daniel said, like she had reserved this request for a time when she would really need it. 'How can anyone make that decision? Like, why would you just give up like that?'

For fear of providing an answer that Daniel didn't want to hear, I instead nodded and urged him to continue.

'She kept mentioning it after that and I kept telling her that it wasn't an option. Then you came along.' He paused and fashioned an expression that may have been construed as loving or admiring under different circumstances.

'What did I have to do with any of this?' I asked, feeling disproportionately pleased by my alleged involvement.

'She said life moves on and that I'd found someone to spend mine with now.'

Again, under different circumstances, and had I been a normal girl, this would have perhaps been the moment when an extravagant cast of woodland creatures would have poured in through the doors and windows to join me for a musical number. It wasn't quite that reaction, no; I'm no Snow White, after all. But I still struggled to hold back a smile.

Daniel continued with the retelling – of how Emily had repeatedly asked him to help her and how he had repeatedly denied her that – until we got to their most recent discussion, which had taken place a week ago. Daniel and I had been out for the afternoon; Emily's orders. 'The girl is hardly making the most of her summer,' she had said to Daniel, urging him to whisk me away somewhere. I wondered now whether this had somehow been part of her plan.

'She'd been bringing up more and more fluids,' Daniel said, diplomatically referring to the blood and mucus that had to be cleared away from Emily following every cough. 'She knew that things were getting worse, and I did as well, and I was just… worn down, I suppose. Not with her, I don't mean,' he added, quickly, as if trying to save face. 'I was worn down by her asking me to help her, and me running out of ways to actually help her, because I couldn't.' He dropped both hands flat against the table, his head angled towards the wood in a way that allowed him to avoid my stare completely. 'You can't always help. Her medication box.' He lifted his head to gesture towards where it used to live. 'They've taken that as well now. But her box with all the heavy stuff in – Christ, it's so wrong to even talk about this.' He massaged his forehead roughly; the skin turned white from the pressure.

'Daniel, you need to tell me what happened,' I said, desperate for the details.

'I told her that I couldn't do it. I'm weak, and I couldn't. But if she wanted to, if she really felt like that was what she needed to do, then she could take extra. From the box.'

The soliloquy continued but was disturbed by repeated apologies and growing sobs that became so violent I was concerned Daniel may slip into a panic attack. 'I killed her. I killed her, and I have to be okay with that and I don't even know how–'

I kissed him, hard, to catch his confession. He was half-right. He hadn't killed her, exactly, so much as allowed her to die. But there was still something quite wonderful about it all.

Chapter twenty

It had been a few days since Daniel's confession. We were spending much of our time together, and yet somehow we managed to navigate around the most obvious topic of conversation quite masterfully. It became harder to leave him for any substantial period of time, but the human body requires a certain amount of nutritional input to maintain an adequate standard of functioning. Eventually I abandoned the nest we had made for ourselves in the living room – which I had previously only left to return home and sleep – and ventured out to the supermarket. When I was close to the entrance of the shop, that's when I saw her.

She maintained the same military stature that I had seen during our last encounter. Her rear end was planted on the floor, her feet a perfect distance apart. Each ear stood to attention, upright and alert, waiting for him. I looked at the bowed heads of busy shoppers wandering past us, ignorant, and I wondered – would anyone even stop me? Would he berate himself for leaving her when he came back to find she was gone? I bit back on the urge. It was impractical. With the recent influx of excitement that had impacted my daily routines, I had completely neglected to keep track of Paul's. Of course he would be there. Where else would they be on a Tuesday afternoon? I glanced down at my watch: 2:38pm. Daniel had robbed me of much of my free time recently. I had neglected so many opportunities with Paul and, nursing a flutter of something at the thought of seeing him again, I only now realised how much I had missed my time with him. Calculating the approximate length of his shopping excursion, I realised that I had to grasp at this chance while it was there. I walked back to my car, started the engine, and followed the quickest route from the supermarket back out towards Prescott Lane. Paul was a relatively intelligent individual and yet, in the weeks before Emily's death, I had been truly incapable of grasping the security measures – or lack thereof – that he took with his home. Peaches may have endowed him with a sense of security but she was an ineffective tool in that respect given Paul's increasing tendency to remove her from the house every time he went out himself. However, Peaches' determined appearance aside, she was an almost entirely wasted measure given that Paul was yet to replace the lock on his back gate that had recently been broken, and, as it turned out, he wasn't particularly wary about unlocked windows either. Through the pane, the upturned lock mechanism was easily visible and, with a slim enough implement and the proper leverage–

The window opened with an understated click. I perched on the ledge and lifted one leg then the other through the frame. My previous guesswork had been right; this was the utility room. And so, curious about what I might actually find buried around the house, I wandered without urgency from one room to the next, as if I had just bought the place rather than having just broken in.

The kitchen was clinical. The living room was understated and modern, with highlights of chrome scattered liberally throughout, and I was disproportionately pleased to see that my guesswork on Paul's wooden flooring was right. The dining room was unloved, housing nothing more than brown boxes that held the promise of furniture, with a backdrop of garden that could be seen through the patio doors. The garden itself was immaculate, with a lawn neatly shaved into strips of light and shade.

'Anything for Peaches,' I said to the empty space. But I stalled in the hallway.

On a waist-high unit at the bottom of the stairs there was a framed photograph. A slightly younger version of Paul stood proudly inside the frame, suited and smiling with an arm hanging around the shoulder of an uncomfortably pretty brunette positioned next to him. His fingertips were digging into her shoulder. Her smile didn't reach her eyes. Was this the woman that he had told me about? They were familiar with each other, clearly, but I couldn't comfortably tie them together in a romantic relationship from this image. Just an old friend, perhaps, or his sister even seemed more likely. I wondered what had happened immediately before this photograph was taken, and why Paul would want a snapshot memory of feelings so evidently forged.

Abandoning the image on the unit, I moved upstairs. I found the spare bedroom disguised as an office, the bathroom – which was where I'd suspected it would be – and then finally Paul's bedroom. The double bed was neatly made but I was only midway through inspecting his hospital corners when something distracted me. On Paul's nightstand there was another image, this one of Paul kissing someone who appeared to be the same brunette from downstairs – not his sister, then – although I couldn't be too definitive about that. Her face was hidden by his but her frame was similar. A happier memory, from what I could see. But I still didn't understand why it was there.

There was an elaborate dog's bed – designed with the appearance of a bed that would belong to a human – in one corner, and a double wardrobe, doors still wide open, in the corner opposite. This wardrobe was entirely full of shirts, organised according to colour so that the display ran as a spectrum from crisp white to almost black. I ran my hand across their edges.

I hadn't seen Paul in a shirt once. Not even on the mornings he left without Peaches. Despite planning to leave the room, I was drawn towards the bed. Lying down, I manoeuvred myself into the exact position that I imagined Paul must sleep in, as estimated by the positioning of his pillows. From this angle, there was nothing in what would have been his eyeline. No television, no books. Instead he had a clear view of where Peaches would lie, one head tilt away from the woman who occupied his nightstand. After taking another glance at the photograph – is that what Paul looked at, before he went to sleep? – I buried my face into his pillow. The case was scented by aftershave and perspiration. My nose chased after a flicker of cigarettes that I couldn't pin to Paul's character, unless, perhaps like the shirts, that behaviour was reserved for when I wasn't there to observe it.

Back downstairs I made an inventory, of sorts. The smells attached to the sofa, the knives readily available in the kitchen, the amount of locks on the front door. I wanted to know the inside of the house as well as I knew the outside, but I had already misplaced nearly an hour in Paul's home, and he would be back no later than 4:30pm. Assuming, of course, that he'd driven (there was no car in the drive) and that he had stopped to stretch Peaches' legs somewhere on the way home (which was their usual habit on a Tuesday afternoon). On my walk back to the utility room I considered taking something; something inconsequential that Paul would hardly notice. I shook away images of a shirt, a small knife, and found myself distracted then by a stuffed animal. It had been discarded in the middle of the kitchen floor – it was battered and no larger than an apple. Paul had only bought this for Peaches about a month ago, in the early days of our excursions. He had been caught between this and a more robust-looking plastic hamburger. I thought – as I had done originally – that Paul would have been better off having purchased this second option. Peaches was a beast, after all.

The toy seemed like the safest choice, but there was a more useful utensil that caught my eye as I walked back through the kitchen, and it was tempting. I ran a thumb over what I thought must be a spare key to the front door, left discarded on the kitchen work surface. There was a key ring attached – the type that comes hollow, for you to force your own picture inside – that had a snapshot of a young Peaches in the frame. I hadn't noticed it on my first walk through; there had been nothing that I wanted, or needed particularly, from the experience after all. I had come here primarily out of curiosity, I suppose, although that had ebbed on the journey around Paul's personal space. But how long until the curiosity reappeared? A theft – an actual crime – felt like a step in a very serious direction and I wondered, briefly, whether

I was ready for it. Time was a factor, and it seemed unlikely that an opportunity quite this good would wander by me again and so I pocketed the key, feeling something between excitement and trepidation in my gut as I did so.

I left through the same unlocked window that had allowed me entry and pushed it closed behind me. The gate knocked when I pulled it shut but, cautious of being spotted, or worse still recognised, I resisted the urge to look around for anyone who may have acknowledged the noise. My car was parked three streets away and so I set off towards it with the sun in my face, a spring in my step, and a heartbeat that was audible. The latter only quickened more when I saw a car – theirs, not mine – travelling in my direction at a pace that was lower than the speed limit. It was Paul's way, it seemed, when Peaches was in the car with him.

He wasn't completely clear from this angle, but Peaches' head – which was hanging from the passenger window – was impossible to miss. I observed her, smiled – I may have even laughed, I can't quite remember – and then turned my attention elsewhere for the remainder of the walk, as they drove in the opposite direction to me. Inside my car I pulled the key from my pocket and pressed it into my glove compartment. On the way back to the supermarket, I spent the journey practising my best 'Bloody traffic everywhere' before I called Daniel and told him that I was running late. He was kind, as he always was – 'Take your time, GT, there's no need to go rushing around for me' – and for the first time I felt a pang of what I think must have been shame, or at the very least something akin to it.

Chapter twenty-one

It wasn't until the business surrounding Emily's death that I really realised what had been happening with Daniel. It may come as no surprise at all to learn that I had feelings for him and, on reflection, I suspected that they had been blossoming for some time – for want of a less romanticised verb. It was beyond my control. Somehow Daniel and I slipped into a 'you hurt, I hurt' mentality, which was set to be reasonably dysfunctional given how defective we were as humans. Actually, defective may be too strong a word to describe Daniel; he was perfectly well equipped to function adequately around other normal people – but Daniel had a propensity to surround himself with the abnormal. The aunt who wanted to kill herself; the girlfriend who wanted to kill things. Defective? Perhaps not. But there was something unflattering to be said about the company he was keeping.

Daniel, I decided, made me a better human. I could live, breathe, feel through him and that's not to say he fixed me – as though I were only in need of minor repair – but he certainly did pull parts of me in closer. A chemical combination, perhaps, long ago lost by my lizard brain, somehow stitched back together by the archetypal boy next door. Daniel was the Victor to my monster; he breathed humanity (back) into me and I both liked and hated him for it at the same time. But, if I was the monster to Daniel's Frankenstein (which didn't bode particularly well for Daniel, I don't suppose), then Paul was The Vitruvian Man to my da Vinci: a limbs-spread representation of the human body, its proportions, and its capabilities.

How I felt for Paul was how I felt for the rat, the bird, the countless cats that our neighbours had homed despite their total inability to protect them (from me). I wasn't attracted to him so much as I was curious about him. Although Daniel unknowingly did his best to hinder the preoccupation, it became my mission in life to learn the basic formula of Paul's. I studied him – inclined towards afternoon walks; often at home alone during the evenings – how I studied the brown rat. Most likely to enter your garden at night; tempted to climb great lengths to reach bird feeders. He wasn't a romantic interest, no; instead, it felt like he had become a bigger, grander specimen. I wanted to know what made him function, how his life fit together like a jigsaw – what might stop him from working. Paul never did have the Prince Charming effect; he wasn't Daniel.

Daniel was always kind and caring; he thought I was genuinely a worthwhile person – and how wrong he was, as it turned out. But Paul? He was something else altogether.

Chapter twenty-two

'How was the funeral, then?'

My mother's expression remained deadpan as she voiced the question, but something about the phrasing felt jarring. Were there different styles of funeral, I wanted to ask, something other than depressing and overemotional for everyone involved?

The Fault in Our Stars. 2014. Shailene Woodley. 'Funerals, I've decided, are not for the dead. They are for the living.'

I couldn't find an answer to how the funeral was. It may have been heartbreaking – in hindsight that was probably a perfect word to use – but in reality, it seemed to me like an overpriced outpouring of faux affection delivered by names that Emily had never mentioned to me, nor to Daniel. 'There'll be some who just come for the food,' Emily had told me during one of our afternoon talks, and she had been right.

Instead of answering her, I took a step towards my mother and wrapped my arms around her. She remained rigid under the embrace.

'It's horrible to see Daniel like this.'

My mother held her rigidity for a second longer but then relaxed against me, lifting her arms up around me as she did so. We held the embrace for a beat longer than I expected, but eventually it was my mother who pushed me away. She cupped my shoulders with her palms and studied me at arm's length.

'Are you okay?' she asked.

'I will be.'

She nodded in response and then turned back towards the kitchen work surface where she was preparing dinner for us both.

The funeral had taken place earlier that day but Daniel's house had become so overrun with money-hungry relatives – his words, not mine – that I had been forced to vacate in order for him to physically accommodate them.

'I can just go home for a couple of days,' I had told him. Daniel pulled a face at my offer, like the helpful suggestion hindered his predicament rather than assisted with it. 'What's wrong?'

'I'll miss you, idiot.'

The Wizard of Oz. 1939. Judy Garland. 'I think I'll miss you most of all.'

'I'll miss you too,' I lied. Or did I?

I had packed away the few personal items that I'd left scattered around Daniel's spare bedroom, including my experiments box, which was now comfortably hidden beneath a larger-than-necessary-for-this-time-of-year coat in the boot of my car. Daniel had said that I could leave it, that no one would disturb it, but I knew how inquisitive family members could be.

'Funny how quickly things can change, even when they seem relatively stable,' my mother said, bringing me back into the room. She turned, gestured with a carrot, and added: 'With Daniel's aunt, I mean.'

It was an uncomfortable topic to launch a conversation with, particularly after the last time Emily had occupied our dialogue. My mother was yet to address the issue of what we had – or rather, hadn't – spoken about on the night of our dinner with Daniel. But, while she didn't push the issue, it was uncomfortably apparent that she hadn't let it settle either. During our few exchanges there had always been a sense of something unsaid, as if my mother were constantly on the cusp of asking something, saying something, accusing something, but then thought better of it. I wondered whether now would be the time that the real questions were finally asked, or whether my mother's self-control really knew no bounds.

'She did have cancer, Mum,' I said, as if this were an explanation all by itself – which, as far as I was concerned, it should have been.

She sighed. 'Yes, I'm aware of that, Gillian, but it was such a quick turn, that's all.'

It hadn't advanced overnight, I wanted to tell her, before launching into a comprehensive explanation of exactly how these cells develop.

'I think if Daniel is honest with himself then it was just a matter of time before this happened, really.' Daniel and I had discussed what we would tell people when they commented, which they would, on the suddenness of Emily's passing. Overreact, I had told him, overreact and tell them that there's nothing sudden about cancer. 'After all, Mum, there's nothing sudden about cancer, is there?'

My mother arched an eyebrow at the question before turning away again. 'I suppose there isn't, no.'

We continued in this vein for longer than seemed necessary, until much of the information I was giving my mother was recycled from the previous answers I had provided. No one had raised any questions. Yes, she had, technically, been on her own when it happened. 'It's hard to say,' I started. 'Daniel and I might have both been in the house when it happened, but the time of death is a difficult thing to pin down exactly.'

'Did neither of you think to check on the poor woman?'

'Of course we did, Mum. It was when I was checking on her that I realised what had happened and that's when I called for help.'

'You?' my mother asked, more interested now.

'Yes, me. Not Daniel.' I snapped my teeth around his name, eager to protect him. My mother sensed a change in tone and altered her own accordingly.

'Sorry, love. I thought you might want to talk about it.'

'It's all I've talked about since it happened,' I said, which was a lie, of course.

But Daniel and I had talked about lots of things around the topic of Emily. For the first twenty-four hours after her death we discussed her at length. When it happened, how it must have happened, how horrid it was that it had happened at all. We anticipated questions, drafted our answers, and we nursed our guilt in between. Sorry, no. Daniel nursed his guilt in between. There was no need for us both to feel it, I thought.

The Machinist. 2004. Christian Bale. 'A little guilt goes a long way.'

'I wondered – worried,' my mother said, correcting herself. 'How it might impact you, with what happened to your dad.'

'She's Daniel's relative, Mum.'

'I know that, Gillian, but you only recently lost a relative of your own,' she said, but then sighed, as though disappointed by her own bluntness.

Attending two funerals over the course of one summer was not quite how I had imagined my time at home would play out, I'll admit. The link she was making still felt tenuous. It was clear she was moving somewhere with this. After too much silence on my part my mother turned to look at me and found me frowning over her response. Returning to the peeling, chopping, whatever she was doing, she added: 'Bit close for comfort, love, that's all I meant.'

The comment didn't clarify anything so much as complicate it further.

'I see.'

'How are you feeling about things now?'

The question was on the tip of her tongue long before I had even decided on my own non-committal reply. And this, I thought, must have been the reason for the link: she wanted to discuss feelings.

'I try not to think about Dad, if I'm honest, Mum.'

My mother prepared the rest of dinner in such a determined silence that I wondered – or perhaps hoped – that the conversation had fallen from her head. She finished dicing, successfully boiled and mashed as appropriate, and even wandered to and from our utility room with washed and to-be-washed clothes without uttering anything in the vein of a response. But when she set the food-laden plate down in front of me, I realised she had been saving this talk for the intimacy of dinner.

'Gillian, do you really never think about what happened?'

That's not what I said, I thought, as I threw a sizeable chunk of chicken into my mouth to buy myself thinking time. Did we always have to have these conversations over, or immediately after, the consumption of food? I wanted to ask. Did my mother not appreciate how indigestion worked?

'Of course I do.' I maintained eye contact with my plate. It hadn't escaped my attention that my mother had more roast potatoes than I did and I was disproportionately irritated about that. 'I wouldn't be normal if I didn't think about it, would I?'

'I just thought that all of this with Emily might have brought some things up.'

'They're hardly similar situations, Mum.'

'Aren't they?' she asked. I frowned into my dinner, confused by her insinuation, and she must have noticed. 'Death is death, isn't it? That's all I meant,' she added. But it wasn't all.

I speared chicken, a carrot, and a potato one after the other and threw the medley into my mouth before I could say anything inappropriate or damning. The companionship I shared with Daniel had evolved into something that allowed us to say (almost) anything to each other. My mother and I, however, had no such relationship, and I compartmentalised those two states before saying: 'I'm not sure death is death. That makes the whole thing sound quite inconsequential.'

'Don't do that, Gillian.' Her response was firm. I thought she must have been ready with it for some time, depending on what I contributed to this talk. 'You're being clinical again.' A fine criticism, I thought, from someone who had boiled death down to a simple and derivative process. 'All I'm asking is whether it's brought any feelings up for you,' she finished.

'And it hasn't.'

'Well good, because that's all.'

We both knew it wasn't all, but it would have to do for now.

'So Daniel has family there at the moment?' she asked between mouthfuls.

'Mm – not his parents, though.' I spoke around a mouthful of over-boiled carrots, knowing my mother would fill the silence should I wait too long to respond. 'Which I think is peculiar. Emily was related to one of them, after all, and your parents should be there for you during difficult periods in your life,' I said, unaware of the accidentally snide comment that I had just made about my own parents, more driven by my protective feelings for Daniel. My mother had noticed the potential malicious remark.

'What's that meant to mean?'

'Well, you'd think his family would support him.'

'Even families have to draw a line, Gillian. We can't always support you.'

It felt like we were discussing something else now.

'Mum, is everything okay?' I asked, trying a different tactic.

She considered the question for longer than seemed necessary before offering an unconvincing 'Yes, love' and returning to her meal.

'I feel like there's something you want to say but you aren't saying it,' I pressed. I was being stifled by this elephant in the room, one that now seemed to be swelling at an alarming rate. I was gripped by a sudden need to gun it down, gut it, and harvest its ivory.

My mother placed her knife and fork down either side of her plate and finished chewing with slow and deliberate movements. She swallowed and rubbed at her eyes, giving over an expression of exasperation, or maybe tiredness, and said: 'I've got a lot on my mind at the moment, Gillian.'

My time with Daniel had well-informed me about what came next on my part. 'Would you like to talk about it, Mum?'

I can't be sure – it was just a flicker, really – but I think that she flinched.

'Gillian, what did you do with the box?'

My face, despite my best efforts to hold back, must have looked startled. It hadn't been the starting point that I was anticipating and I now found myself reassessing what it was that my mother was worrying about, for this to be her chosen point on which to build whatever came next. I thumbed through stock responses, frantically looking for an answer, when it occurred to me that they were hazardous. The animals, that is, not the answers I was looking through. It wasn't a case of simply hauling them into a non-recycling bin. Would my mother know that?

Even so, could I risk her knowing that?

'They're in the boot of my car.'

She definitely flinched then, as if she were physically pained by the answer.

'Why are they there, Gillian? Why didn't you get rid of them?' Her tone was measured and controlled but taut, as she held back the emotion that threatened to crack through.

'They're hazardous. Technically. I can't just throw them in a bin.'

'So how can you get rid of them?'

'To be honest, Mum, I don't really know.' And why should I have known? It never occurred to me that I would need to get rid of them. 'When I'm back at university I can ask one of my lecturers, or maybe even dispose of it through the university.'

She closed her eyes, shook her head slightly. 'That's not good enough.'

Nothing ever is, I thought, feeling an unfamiliar stab of bitterness towards her.

'What do you want me to do?'

'Your lecturers have emails, don't they?'

I nodded, understanding her implication. 'I'll email one of them first thing in the morning to see whether they can advise me on the matter.' I flinched at my own tone, noting how clipped it was a little too late to edit it. With the final roast potato left on my plate I chased around a dribble of gravy, dabbing the liquid into the food before tucking it into my mouth. When my mother didn't offer any further remarks, I pushed a little harder: 'Is there anything else that's on your mind?'

'Plenty.'

'I'm here to talk, if you feel like expanding.'

She spat out a puff of air, rolled her eyes, and shook her head in rapid succession.

'I don't know what that means, Mum.'

A similar gesture followed but this one was accompanied by the rattle of cutlery as she placed utensils on the plate in front of her. She had left two roast potatoes, and I tried to not be aggravated by this as she pushed the plate towards me, indicating that it was my duty to do the washing up. I made off in the direction of the sink, which was already stuffed with various pans and paraphernalia. So much so, in fact, that I wondered whether my mother had created such a mound in an attempt to keep me out of her way for a while, but I shook the thought away as idle paranoia. I was midway through filling the washing up bowl full of water when my mother spoke again, in such a quiet tone that I had to turn off the tap and ask her to repeat her remark.

'I said: I'll be ready to talk soon, I think.'

And then she left, saying something about an early night, and needing the extra rest.

Chapter twenty-three

Louise's office was a medley of smells. There was tomato, garlic, coffee, perfume. I had interrupted her lunch and I thought I should feel a stab of guilt, or something, for that. But I was also sure that at some point – despite not being an actual doctor, I know – Louise must have taken one oath or another where she solemnly swore to protect her clients from harm. It was, perhaps, disingenuous to use this in my bargaining to see her. I wasn't in harm's way, I didn't think. But I couldn't be sure that someone else wasn't. The receptionist had asked whether it was an emergency. A moot question, I thought, given that I was standing directly in front of her having arrived unannounced without an appointment demanding to see my therapist – which shortly gave way to pleas of, failing that, any therapist at all. *Does it look like an emergency?* I wanted to ask her. *Are these not urgent actions?*

'She said she'll see you now if you pop down,' the woman said after hitting several keys on her laptop. No sooner had she uttered the sentence I was gone.

We sat in our usual positions on opposing sofas. Louise wiped at the corners of her mouth, inspected her thumbs – presumably for any remnants of food that she had just wiped away – then dropped her hands, folded, into her lap. She was evidently waiting for me to say something but she hadn't given me anything to answer.

She sighed, uncrossed and then re-crossed her legs, and said: 'Do you want to tell me what's wrong, Gillian?'

I tilted my head left and then right as if attempting to shake an answer loose. 'I think it's my mother.'

'Okay. Has something in particular happened with your mother?'

I performed the same head shift as before but nothing came out this time. I wasn't aware of anything particular having happened with her, no. But I nevertheless felt certain that she was the reason I had needed to see Louise. Since Emily's funeral my attachment to my mother had slackened, for want of a better phrase, while the attachment I felt towards Daniel was growing stronger by the day. So much so that too much physical proximity from him sometimes gave me literal heartache – romanticised phrasing for anxiety, of course, but still.

Despite our distance – or perhaps because of it – my mother had in fact been making what seemed like a determined effort to redress the balance of communication in our household. She cooked dinner for us both, sometimes for Daniel as well. She suggested that she and I should spend more time together, and she made an effort to maintain a conversation even when my ability to feign interest in such a thing had long faded. But she also asked, on an almost daily basis, how exactly I was feeling about 'things' – she was never more specific about what she was asking, but there was always an undertone of something suspicious beneath the question – and, in addition to this, it had not gone unnoticed that she checked my room intermittently. For tiny carcasses, I thought, with more amusement than I should have felt. Nothing had happened, no, but I couldn't stifle the feeling that something was about to.

'There's something in the pit of my stomach that I don't recognise.'

'Something, meaning a feeling?'

I nodded.

'And it's not a feeling you've had before?'

'Not that I can recall.'

She paused here to make a note of something.

'Talk me through it, Gillian. What is the feeling like, what does it remind you of?'

Every phrase that I tried to wrap around the sensation sitting in my lower abandon felt like an uncomfortable cliché. It was the dip in a rollercoaster, there was an eager beaver in my stomach – something that was champing at the bit, bouncing off the walls, with bells on, on the cusp of hitting fever pitch. I pulled the words around me, scratched at them like they were cheap fabric, and then I stripped them away, discarded them on the floor, leaving a trail of intangible feelings behind me as I paced Louise's office, incapable of sitting still.

Interiors. 1978. Mary Beth Hurt. 'I feel the need to express something, but I don't know what it is I want to express. Or how to express it.'

'It might not be about my mother.'

She nodded.

'Okay, what else could it be about?'

'Someone I felt close to died recently,' I said, reaching for the first thing I could find.

'I'm sorry to hear that, Gillian. I assume we're not talking about your father here?'

'I said someone I felt close to,' I snapped, instantly regretting the remark.

'Gillian, I want you to close your eyes for me.'

I cocked an eyebrow at her suggestion. An almost-laugh escaped her and left behind the traces of a smirk. She set the pen and paper down alongside her in its usual spot, uncrossed her legs, and leaned forward so that her elbows were balanced against her knees.

'Trust me?' she said. And so I did. I leaned back against the welcoming cushions that were wedged on the sofa and I closed my eyes.

'I want you to breathe. But not normal breathing. I want you to inhale for me, and hold it until I tell you otherwise.'

And so I did. I pulled in a greedy amount of air as if fearing that this may be the last time I would have the opportunity to do so. My chest expanded until my once-slouched position was nearly upright as my lungs flooded. In the dead silence of the office, I could just about hear Louise counting – 'One, two, three, four, five, six' – before she said: 'And exhale for me, Gillian.' We repeated the process for longer than I realised at the time, although I remember thinking that these were likely to be the most expensive breaths I had ever taken, would ever take. When Louise was satisfied with my efforts, she said: 'Without thinking too much about your answer now, I want you to keep your eyes closed, and I want you to tell me why you're here.'

'Daniel. I'm here because of Daniel.'

I hadn't thought about the answer, but immediately after spitting it out my eyes snapped open with the startled expression of a cat on the cusp of being garrotted. *Where did that come from?* I thought. Between Louise's questions and my non-committal answers, we spent the remainder of the session trying to work out just that.

'Gillian, is this your first boyfriend?'

'He isn't a boyfriend.'

'No? Then what is he?'

I considered this, and then begrudgingly admitted defeat. 'Okay, he's a boyfriend.'

'So this dynamic isn't something that you've had before?'

'No,' I said, again begrudgingly.

'Is it one that you find easy, or could this perhaps be a source of the struggle here?'

I considered this for a second. It hadn't been easy, no. 'It might have been easier if Daniel were the only man in my life.'

'There's another man in your life?' Louise probed. Understandably so, I had just announced what I imagined to be a conventionally gossip-worthy piece of information, but I instantly felt like I should have kept it to myself. 'Are you romantically involved with this other man, too?'

'No, I don't think so.'

'So, what is your relationship with this other person? Physical?'

A penny dropped. Yes, it was physical. That was exactly what it was.

'How often do you see this other man?'

'As often as I can, around Daniel.'

'Surely that's a source of conflict?'

'It can be, especially with time.'

In the four days before this meeting I hadn't been able to see Paul at all, because I hadn't been able to leave Daniel. Not that I hadn't wanted to leave but more that I couldn't bring myself to; one need outweighed the other, but it was only temporary. I could never make it stick. There was a peculiar out-of-sight feeling with Daniel now – when I was with him, the thought of leaving was uncomfortable. But when I wasn't with him, I didn't always feel like I needed to be.

'Do you expect to always feel that way?' Louise picked.

'I don't know.'

'And this other man, do you always need to be around him?'

'No. But I'd like to spend more time learning about him.'

Louise scribbled something down ahead of saying: 'That's interesting, Gillian.' She paused to write something else down, suddenly latching onto an additional piece of information, then she continued in a different vein: 'And this distance with your mother, this has coincided with this new relationship – relationships, rather. Do you think that could be anything to do with this?'

'Why?'

'Because we grow up, Gillian, and we move away from our parents as we experience life away from them. We're independent entities, aren't we?' It hadn't previously been Louise's style but there was something slightly too kumbaya about her current perspective and it made me nervous. 'Perhaps we can discuss how this impacts you and your mother next time. If the focus is on Daniel, and this other person, then I'm interested in unpacking that further.'

'I have these urges,' I found myself admitting to her, some thirteen minutes later when Louise had finished with her stream of carefully constructed questions. They must have been effective, I thought, because I was suddenly outpouring feelings I had previously been unaware that I even harboured. 'I have these urges and I've never had anything like it and I don't understand where they're coming from or what I'm meant to do with them. And it feels wrong, I think, to act on them or to consider acting on them because is that behaviour actually allowed? Really? Or am I trying to convince myself it is, because it's obviously deep-seated in the human psyche to such an extent that I'm feeling it, so, does that by default make the whole thing natural somehow, normal even?'

Louise looked at me sympathetically, as an older sister or perhaps even a mother might look at their younger female relative. 'I think I understand what you're talking about here, Gillian.'

I was glad she did because I just wasn't sure any more.

'These urges. Who do you feel them for?'

I thought, harder than I'd thought about all of this before, and I searched for what felt like an authentic and accurate answer.

'They're both different, I think.'

Louise nodded and smiled, like she had been expecting this. 'And I think that's probably where our conflict lies. You're a young and healthy woman. These urges that you're feeling, they're completely natural, and I'm sure you know that deep down, don't you?' She cocked her head, craning for a view of my expression that was angled away from her. 'Part of the problem is that you're not controlling these urges properly, because you don't know where to direct them. Does that sound fair?'

I nodded. Not so much in agreement, but rather curiosity.

'There are a lot of changes going on your life, and Daniel's, from what you've told me of him, but you actually sound like you're very good for each other. You've never opened up like this before, about him, and surely that's a sign of something positive.'

I wanted to ask why but she pushed on again before I could.

'This other person. What function are they serving, right now, apart from complicating your relationship with Daniel?'

I flicked to Daniel then, his floppy hair and his lazy smile. And then I flicked to Paul.

Peaches. The house. The unlocked window.

I shook my head.

'Take your time, Gillian.'

'You're saying that I should get rid of the other person?' I asked, knowing that it was an unfair question, but somehow not caring. Perhaps because I knew what her answer would be.

She smiled and said: 'If you don't need them, or want them, particularly, then why keep them?'

***

Daniel had told me that he had an open-door policy. He had even mentioned giving me a key but at my request had refrained from it. It was just another thing for me to lose, I'd told him, and that was an adequate half-reason at least. Truthfully, it had felt like a clash of commitments somehow when Daniel thrust a spare house key in my face some two hours after I had taken Paul's.

When I'd finished with Louise I went straight home, skirted around my mother's questions – 'It went fine, we just talked about Daniel, actually' – and I packed a bag. My mother didn't ask where I was going. She had already assumed that I would be going to Daniel's, because where else would I have been going?

When Daniel opened the door some thirty minutes later he was clearly surprised, and I thought then that an open-door policy must mean something different to the two of us. His eyebrows were arched and his smile slightly less pronounced than I was accustomed to seeing it, but before I could pick up on either of these traits Daniel beat me to speech.

'This is a nice surprise,' he started, stepping aside in the doorway as a signal for me to move inside the house. 'Did we have something planned?'

'No, I don't think so.'

'Coming in?' he asked, noting my fixed position on the doorstep.

'I'd like to stay over tonight, if that would be okay.'

He nodded towards the bag. 'I had guessed that was where you were going with this,' he said, pausing for a half-laugh. 'I told you, you're always welcome. The spare bedroom is made up.'

Something pulled at the corner of my lips; a thought, or a feeling, dragging my mouth down into an expression of deliberation. Daniel caught the look and lowered himself into my eyeline. His face was a silent plea for me to speak but I needed a second to formulate the thought. I flicked through film references but couldn't find the right memory for it and I was unsure of how it should come out, whether it should be forward or understated, whether I should try to sound nervous.

Was I nervous?

'I'd like to stay in your bedroom, if that would be okay. With you, I mean.'

Suspicion. 1941. Cary Grant. 'I think I'm falling in love with you, and I don't quite like it.'

Chapter twenty-four

The last time I looked at the clock it was 1:38am. I waited for another two, perhaps even three, minutes but then decided that I really did need to leave. It wasn't Daniel, as such. Actually, perhaps partly Daniel, at a push. He was an enthusiastic sleeper, snorer, cuddler. In many ways the latter was what I had silently agreed to when I got into his bed instead of my own, but I hadn't realised the full extent of the physical contact – after the *other* kind of physical contact, that is – that happened when two people slept alongside each other. It was, arguably, naivety on my part, and had I not felt such a persistent need to be elsewhere then I might well have enjoyed the moments when I would start to drift off and, quite out of nowhere, a hand would land on my arm, stomach, thigh, as if Daniel were checking that I was still there. I pulled up my underwear and jeans in one motion. While searching the room for signs of my clothing from the night before, I couldn't help but imagine the medley of surprise and panic Daniel would feel the next time he reached over to the other side of the bed. His imagined reaction was nearly enough to make me stay. Only nearly.

Fully clothed again I turned to grab one last look at him and, for another second, I thought maybe I shouldn't leave. Maybe I should put this out of my head and, like a normal girl, spend the night in bed with her boyfriend after a near-satisfying bout of shared physical intimacy. It was my first time – Daniel's first time – being intimate with someone; our first time waking up next to each other seemed a natural conclusion to that. But there was still an ache, an itch that I couldn't reach – and I couldn't believe that was anything to do with what Daniel and I had done. It was far too familiar a feeling for that.

The house was a different playground entirely at that time of the morning. Streetlights crept in through the windows like non-discreet burglars trying to case the hallway for access points, and as I paced around, half-convinced that I might still be able to talk myself out of what was coming, I felt as if the light followed me. From one room to the next, the dim interrogation lamps fell through the windows, catching at my face on occasion. The longer they persisted the more pronounced their imagined questions became to me, asked without the urgency that they really required under such circumstances. *Are you sure you want to do this? Are you really going to make this happen?*

Daniel had two sets of knives in his kitchen. There was the set wedged neatly into the light wooden block that lived on his work surface, and there were the harsher, rougher ones that lived inside the kitchen drawer, beneath the sink and to the left. I ran my fingers over the plastic handles that were sticking out of the blocked set and I remembered:

'Do you even like cheese?' Daniel had asked, knife in hand, his back towards me.

'It depends on the cheese.'

A snort of air had escaped him as he shook his head.

'What an answer. Okay, GT, easier question. Do you want cheese on your sandwich, or not so much?' He'd turned to face me then, revealing a light-hearted smile and a sizeable wedge of cheddar that was lying on the counter behind him.

I'd nodded, smiled in return. 'Okay, cheese and ham sandwiches it is then.'

I could even remember the knife that he'd used.

The drawer – beneath the kitchen sink and to the left – played host to a range of potentially dangerous implements which were, of course, intended for cooking preparation. There were possibilities, I thought, as I ran my fingers across the handles that were messily bunched together at the bottom end of the space. I stalled at one handle, slightly larger than the others, attached to a carving knife.

'Do you want me to do that?' I'd asked Daniel on seeing him fumble about with the blade. 'I don't want you to hurt yourself, Daniel.'

'Christ, Gillian, emasculating much?' He turned to assess my face but on seeing my blank expression he softened. 'I am man. Man carve meat. Woman eat meat,' he said, in mock caveman tones that balanced out the bitter snap of his previous response. 'It'll be fine. What's the worst that can happen?'

'You cut yourself?'

'Now if that's the absolute worst, I reckon we'll be alright.'

I remembered how he'd cut the meat, clumsily digging the blade in this way and that, desperately trying to get a better score on the crisped skin.

'Okay, so, I can't cut meat.' Daniel had eventually admitted, dropping the knife with a light clang on the kitchen work surface. 'You're up, GT.'

The meat had fallen away from the bone. Daniel just didn't know what he was doing with a knife. And I remember thinking what a good thing that probably was.

Shaking off the memory, I grabbed a tea towel from the kitchen work surface and, after pulling the carving knife from the drawer, I secured the blade inside a doubled-up stretch of the fabric. After that, I marched. Out of the house, through the streets, towards Runner's Route, with a determination that suggested I knew where I was going – and I suppose, by then, I had already decided on an end destination. The time had rolled somewhere beyond 2am. Paul would be asleep, as would Peaches, I hoped, although I had no way of knowing for certain. She could have been roaming, she could have been a barker, eagerly waiting for the sound of an intruder before alerting her owner. But it didn't seem to matter much by that point. With the bound blade tucked underneath my arm I pressed forward, pausing only briefly to eye something slumped on one of the benches in the park.

The man's head was bent so low towards the top of his chest that his neck was barely visible. At that angle, streaks of light from the streetlamps were bouncing about on the bald patch on top of his head, which could be seen through the hole in his hat. On closer inspection it became clear that the man was made up entirely of hole-ridden clothes, right down to the shoes, both of which had small and blackened toes sticking out from their fronts. His feet were guarding what appeared to be near-empty bottles of cheap liquor; I wondered if he'd kept them for their sentimental value. The body rose and deflated with breaths that were so laboured they were almost snores. And I wondered for a second whether this person would be better. Whether Paul deserved what was about to happen to him. Whether deserving it had anything to do with it at all. Which it didn't, of course. I did realise that eventually.

The Godfather: Part II. 1974. Al Pacino. 'If anything in this life is certain, if history has taught us anything, it is that you can kill anyone.'

The homeless man was an opportunity, yes, but not quite the one that I was looking for. I passed by him and continued through the streets, surprised at how many houses were lit at what I thought to be fairly antisocial hour. When I rounded the corner onto Prescott Lane, there was only one house that still had lights bouncing around its innards. On the thirty-minute walk I had constructed, deconstructed, and reimagined one possibility after another for how the following events may play out; I even berated myself for leaving Paul's key in my car – for all the use that it would ever be there – before soothing myself with the knowledge that, as far as I had seen, he still hadn't repaired the back gate. It hadn't occurred to me that of all the ways in which this could go wrong, Paul still being up and about in the middle of the night was a genuine possibility.

Dim lights were dotted around the house – various table lamps, I thought, used to light one hallway or another – while the main light was tumbling out of the living room. Whatever Paul was doing, he hadn't even closed the curtains. I could have, should have, left. But somehow, even then, it all still seemed worth the risk.

Edging around the house I eventually stood alongside the frame of the living room window, taking deep breaths in and exhaling to steady myself while I attempted to formulate some kind of action. The original plan might still work. Paul being awake, alert – it hardly seemed to matter. Because I was outside his house and I knew what I was doing and I knew how I was going to do it and the basic plan was still very much in place – until I looked through the window. I couldn't recognise her from the angle she was at, her face dipped down towards Paul, but I felt certain that she wasn't the brunette from the photographs; the shade of her hair was all wrong. Paul was sitting on the floor in front of the sofa while she sat behind him, her legs open enough for him to have shuffled back in between her thighs. His head rolled around in what I assumed was enjoyment as she kneaded at his shoulder blades. Paul's reactions slowed as the woman paused to unbutton his shirt.

So this was who Paul saved his shirts for.

I watched as she ran her fingers over his chest and then back down over his shoulders, before eventually settling around his neck area. She felt around his clavicle, shifting muscle and skin in such clumps that it looked mouldable, and I lost track of how long I watched them like this. I pulled in a sharp breath as her fingertips settled on his laryngeal prominence; they hovered there for a second longer than I thought they should have done but then she continued on her path down his body. When I let my breath go, the air stuttered out of me.

Jealousy is disgusting, isn't it?

Chapter twenty-five

I gave them another ten minutes while I assessed my options, observed their apparent intimacy. The woman, whoever she was, was only half Paul's size. Her frame naturally petite, she clearly wasn't inclined towards developing her muscular strength. I could take her. It would be easy enough to wrap eight fingers round her neck and press two thumbs, hard, against her windpipe. But what would Paul be doing? It seemed unlikely that he would leave me to go about my business. Likewise, I couldn't quite imagine this woman standing still and waiting her turn. The whole evening had already been a risk, but this would be too much.

When I backed away from the window – from their display – there was something that resembled a sinking feeling in my chest cavity; the sensation you experience when it takes longer than usual to find your car keys, or when you realise that you haven't replied to an important email. I couldn't watch any more, but it was hardly like there was somewhere else that I could be. I could have gone back to Daniel, I suppose, but I didn't trust this feeling with him and so I walked, kept walking…

The pavement was bloodied; small clots of something pressed flat and then smudged away. It took longer than it should have done for me to realise that these marks were squashed berries. There were one or two full-bodied survivors dotted along the side of the road. I imagined them with emotions that didn't belong to them: shock and abject horror. I had to do something with the feelings. Seven steps later there was a crunch underfoot that stopped me. A partially flattened beer can was wedged underneath my boot; two steps along there was another empty can, and three steps beyond that, there were people still drinking. A group of them – only just younger than me – were spilling from the front garden of a half-lit house, sporting cigarettes and slurred sentiments.

'You're so special to me, man.'

I was a full three streets away from Paul's house by now. It was a built-up area but the drunks didn't seem to mind. Their conversations increased in volume and I worried for their neighbours.

'I'm not even drunk.'

'You are.'

'Am not.'

I crossed the road to avoid pushing through the cracks in their group.

'Ask her!'

The instruction was slurred. I didn't turn around but I was instantly aware of the words dribbling in my direction. *Don't ask me*, I wanted to tell them. *I don't know anything.* I quickened my pace to get away from them, slowing only when their voices became indiscernible. It took a full two streets. I was surprised that no one had called the police, reported their disruption – but that wasn't an action that I was going to initiate. I had seen enough of the police for one summer.

In the minutes that followed I walked with determination, compulsively even, as if I could outrun what had happened earlier. I focused on the inane and replaced counting seconds with counting streets; houses with their lights on; how many lights to a house. Grange Road had seven households still awake; Manor Road, five; The Crescent, just two. The lights deteriorated and soon so did the houses, replaced by pavement, empty roads, and over-hanging trees – too-dark stretches where streetlights should have been. I buried my hands in my pockets, lowered my head, pressed forward as though I knew where I was going; I don't think I had decided by then – that came in the minutes after.

There were another three streets coming up, the first of which was a matter of twenty short steps away now: Orchard Gardens (four households awake), Winsdor Road (two), Hurst Lane (three). There was a car pulling out from Hurst Lane when I arrived; one male driver. I paused on the footpath while he looked left, right, and then left again before pulling out onto the main road. When I crossed the junction I looked along the stretch of houses. There was one house awake; three lights in the house; one woman at the end of the drive. She was scantily dressed, her left arm midway in the air like she had just waved the man goodbye.

There was that jealousy again.

It wasn't until I ran out of houses, ran out of streets, that I assessed my options: I could walk home through the park, or I could walk back the way I had just come. Paul and her might have been finished by now – but what difference did that make? The park was a three-minute walk away and there were streetlights every twenty-five steps. During the journey, I slowed in between each light; it felt too interrogatory to stand directly underneath them.

Two minutes away and the air changed. It would have been refreshing under different circumstances but something about this new smell was stale. The pavement became spongy, like the concrete might be about to give way – and part of me wouldn't have minded if it had. The grass banks that framed the pavement to Runner's Route had been cut and their dead trimmings were gathering dew. In the thicker patches the spongy feeling became a bounce.

One minute away from the park and the silence somehow felt denser. It left me wishing for the companionship of the drunken louts, the half-awake houses, the strangers driving home from whatever they had just done to each other. Now I was this close, Runner's Route was the quickest course back home; I had nowhere else to go. But when I stood at the eastern walkway entrance – an entrance I had passed through two dozen times over the summer alone – the dark expanse that stared back looked less familiar, somehow unfriendly, as though the whole place had been taken out of context. Six steps in and the ground at least became more stable; they hadn't cut the grass here yet. Twenty-nine steps in and I wandered, on auto-pilot, along the same path that I had trodden earlier, back towards the homeless waster who I expected to still be there. It took a further eighteen steps for me to notice that my footfalls had developed an echo. Somewhere behind me there were footsteps; company.

I took a tactical pause in the middle of the walkway, prompting a new noise. It was a scraping, a dragging. The sound that appears when something sodden is disturbed.

I clutched the handle of the knife a little tighter, peeled away the protective fabric and held the object close to my chest, before taking a hesitant step forward. Somewhere behind me someone else took a step as well.

My footsteps fell into a run, carrying me towards the streetlight at the edge of the walkway. As my pace increased I became aware of the steel rubbing against my jacket, creating a scrape with each movement. The metronome effect went some way towards pacifying me although I was still counting the seconds between the copycat footfalls. But then I settled under the blinking light. I circled around my safe space, looking for signs of life, maybe even an amused face. Look at the scared little girl – isn't she funny?

I crouched down, knowing that I needed to steady myself. The fingertips of my right hand stretched to the ground and bent uncomfortably under my weight. I inhaled – one, two, three – and exhaled – four, five, six – but I was no longer in a state to steady my breathing. The tacky mess of emotions in my stomach was accompanied by a pain inside my chest now. As I slowly resumed an upright position, I lay my palm flat across my forehead, hoping for a cooling sensation – hoping that I could find reminders of where I was going, and what I would do when I got there, but I was too far gone. The familiar clotting of out-of-control emotions was growing already now – and I could hear them: my mother's accusations; my therapist's optimism; now, perhaps worst of all, Daniel's praise, his panting, his persistent moans of my name.

They were too much, too loud, and only slightly broken down by the footsteps around me, somehow louder now as well.

I changed my grip on the knife as the footsteps quickened into a run. With the implement angled upwards I turned and, as if they were a part of the same movement, raised the knife. I couldn't have known the full force of my movement, nor the full force of his run into me; I couldn't have known that our body differences were so conveniently matched that they left my hand level with his stomach; I couldn't have known that it would be quite this easy.

The Crow. 1994. Laurence Mason. 'Let me tell you about murder. It's fun, it's easy, and you gonna learn all about it.'

The boy collapsed forward onto me. My grip was still tight around the handle as I leaned my weight against him, and he stumbled backwards then, crying out as the other side of the implement was dragged out of him.

He was a kid; six or perhaps seven years younger than me, with a generic hooded appearance that made him seem both unremarkable and indistinct. His eyes grew darker as I watched him, suddenly brimming with tears that might spill over at any minute. I recognised something in that.

The pleas that followed were broken. Grimaces and gasps for air had disturbed the sentence but the meaning was still clear: 'Help, please. Call someone.'

The words were difficult to catch after that. His breathing was deteriorating at an impressive rate as he sank closer to the ground, his body a burst inflatable.

'You should lie down,' I told him. 'If you fall then it might make it worse.'

I pulled my phone from my front pocket.

'Please, I know–'

'I can't get signal here so I need to leave you for a minute, okay? You need to lie flat on your back, I think, and take some deep breaths. Can you do that? And then I'll come back when I've called someone.'

As I moved past him he set a bloodied hand around my ankle. I swallowed the urge to kick him away.

'Promise you'll call for–'

'I promise.'

He loosened his grip. His body hit the ground.

I walked out of the spotlight and into the shadows, my phone in one hand and the knife in the other, as if it had become part of my anatomy. I pressed down on the button at the top of my phone and waited for the screen to light up, in one last kick of life, before extinguishing entirely. I slipped it back into my pocket and looked over to the boy. From this distance he was just a shape, but I could see something sitting on his stomach – his hands, I thought. I imagined him applying pressure, just like the television shows had taught him.

When I rushed back to him his eyes were tightly closed, making his face a grimace. I kneeled down next to him.

'You came.'

'I said that I would.'

'Is someone…?'

The effort that it took him to half-open his eyes was exhausting to observe. Each eyelid fluttered underneath the light like an excited moth. I rested my palm across his forehead, now drenched with sweat, and moved my hand down until it covered his eyes, closing them in one movement. His mouth was now a perfect O as he tried to breathe through the pain. The red patch on his abdomen was much larger than it had been to begin with, his clothing now sodden against his skin. His breathing was barely audible, each exhale somewhere between a light sigh and a wheeze. As he concentrated on getting air in and out of his body, I brushed stray damp hairs away from his forehead.

'Is someone coming?'

I ran my palm over his forehead again until the skin was clear of moisture and then I moved my hand back to his eyes. My palm sat there lightly to begin with, but then I applied pressure, forming a mask over the top half of his face. I felt his eyelashes flutter against my skin as I moved my hand down, slowly, to study the contours of his expression, before coming to a rest over his mouth. His eyes widened, tears tumbling out of their corners now. His arms moved to fight against me but there was hardly much fight left in him at all.

With clenched teeth I leaned forward and left one single kiss on the boy's forehead; his skin was damp with sweat again. When I pulled away from him I allowed myself some time, just a few seconds, to look into his eyes. He breathed heavily against my palm as we watched each other and, quite suddenly, his struggle stopped. It's inappropriate, I think, to think of one person when you're with another, but as if by accident, I thought of Daniel. With this unconscious boy in front of me, and this feeling of complete fulfilment sitting at the base of gut, I thought of Daniel, of what I had done with Daniel, and I realised that this was what had been missing. I kissed the boy's forehead again and, close to his ear, I promised that it would all be over soon. I had convinced myself that it mattered – the who, the when, the how. It didn't. It just mattered that it got done.

Chapter twenty-six

I folded my jeans into a square and placed the knife on top of them. Over the top of that I folded my jacket, also into a square, and then placed the sandwich of evidence in the bottom of my wardrobe. In the shower afterwards the water turned pink as it ran away from me. I

shampooed and rinsed my hair three times to settle the concern that it still harboured a metallic smell, despite the actual levels of foreign iron molecules being barely perceptible after the second wash. When my hair was pinned into a bun I leaned back against the cold tiles and with some relief allowed my knees to buckle beneath me. I slipped down the wall then until I was sitting in the shower bowl, my knees pressed against my chest with my arms pulled tight around them. I tilted my head back, allowing my mass of conditioner-soaked hair to act as a cushion. With my eyes focused on the ceiling I concentrated on breathing, inhaling the steam until parts of me that were previously clogged began to ease open.

Now would be a good time to try it, I remember thinking, and with droplets of water fleeing from the showerhead, I managed to half-convince myself that I'd already started to cry. I jerked my shoulders until they mimicked a heaving motion and I pulled my face into a new expression, too – scrunched-shut eyes and a theatrical frown. After performing these elements in isolation from each other I combined them with my newly, deliberately, laboured breathing, to conjure what I hoped would be an authentic and satisfactory outpouring of emotion.

Half a minute passed before I admitted defeat. I let my fingertips reach up and study the imitated signs of emotion, to catch small balls of water between my thumb and index fingertip and to marvel at them, like they were something miraculous – like they were something I had made. I knew that they weren't, you see, because try as I might when I thought about what I'd done to the boy, I couldn't wipe the smile from my face.

After that shower I slept sounder than I had in months. While tucked away inside my bedroom I was aware of the world now itching to stretch its arms and indulge in a morning yawn outside my window. With the beginnings of sunrise teasing me from behind my closed curtains, I turned, buried my face into my pillow, and slept dreamlessly for four and a half hours until my mother woke me. Her weight dropping onto the bed initially alerted me to her presence and although I had instantly made the decision to ignore her, the curl of her fingers around my upper arm and the gentle shake that followed made it challenging. With my eyes still closed I grumbled at her, feigning more tiredness than I felt in the hope that it would stifle her efforts.

'Gillian?'

'Mm.'

'Love, wake up for me a second.'

'Hmm.'

'Gillian,' she snapped then, apparently losing patience.

'What?'

'Are you okay?'

With both eyes wide open then, I readjusted my position, propped myself upright against my headboard and took a long look at my mother.

'Is that why you woke me up?'

'Yes,' she said without any hesitation or hint that she might be lying. She held my gaze firmly while waiting for a reply but I found myself so stunned, momentarily, that I couldn't actually provide one. 'So? Are you?'

'Yes, Mum, I'm fine, thank you for asking,' I replied after another beat of silence. 'Are you okay?' I asked then, thinking that was the right format to adhere to.

She hesitated. There was a flicker of something across her face but I couldn't decipher what feeling the expression was attached to.

'A young boy was killed last night, not far from here. I thought…' She paused, shook her head, then picked up her sentence in an entirely different place. 'I just wanted to check you were okay, that's all. I heard you come home late, or early, I can't – either way, I just needed to check.'

The Hitchhiker's Guide to the Galaxy. 1981. David Dixon. 'Don't panic… Don't panic.'

I readjusted my position in bed, rubbed at my head and performed a number of other mundane and unnecessary actions to buy myself another second or two, to pull some thoughts together. I lazily settled on: 'That's terrible. Do you know what happened?'

She shook her head.

'I've heard it was a stabbing. Someone found him. In the park. First thing this morning. Some poor dog walker or another.' With each snippet of information that she shared with me she took a glance at my expression, waiting for it to change. I nodded along and only briefly thought of Paul. A disproportionately smug section of my cranium had already edited him and Peaches into the discovery. 'Anyway, as long you're okay.'

She phrased the statement in such a way that it sounded like a question and so I nodded again, giving her a tight smile as I did so.

'I'm fine, just tired.'

She excused herself after that, pulling the door closed behind her while still muttering a promise that she wouldn't disturb me again – 'You do look worn out, Gillian, best to get some rest today.' I couldn't rest after she'd gone. How could I sleep, given the announcement that my mother had just made? This was a living, breathing incident now; people would be discussing it, people would be talking. With my knees pulled up towards me I reached out to my bedside table and found my mobile phone.

You have two new messages.

Daniel: Okay so waking up on my own was a bit surprising. I hope you're okay GT.

Daniel: I hope last night was okay too. Maybe call me when you get this. I'm a bit worried. X

Sorry, I couldn't sleep. Everything is okay. Just can't talk right now.

I wasn't ready for a conversation with Daniel, and that was the chief reason behind my response.

The second reason was that text messages left a better trail than a phone call did.

Daniel: So last night was okay then? Like. I didn't do anything bad?

Last night was one of the most special nights of my life.

Daniel: I can say this over a text easier than to your face so don't judge me okay? I'm so glad that it happened with you. A girl like you I mean. You're pretty damn special.

Daniel: I'm glad that you were my first. X

Alexander Pichushkin, 2007, during his trial as the Chessboard Killer: 'A first killing is like your first love. You never forget it.'

I was glad that he was my first too.

***

When the doorbell rang just over two hours later, I deliberately didn't make a move to answer it. Upstairs in my bedroom, I remained tucked out of sight until I heard a muffled greeting emerge from my mother, and I moved to the top of the stairs then. Perched two steps down, I pulled my knees up towards me, tucked my T-shirt around them, and involuntarily held my breath as Daniel moved into sight. I took a glance at my watch. He was a little earlier than I'd told him to be.

It was a calculated risk, yes, but a risk all the same. Perhaps that went some way towards explaining the abdominal flutter I felt on seeing Daniel, standing in my hallway, unknowingly holding the potential to crush what I had hoped would be my alibi for the previous evening. The plan was balanced delicately on two assumptions. The primary assumption being that my mother, unable to stifle her curiosity – or perhaps her suspicions – would not be able to resist asking Daniel whether I had stayed at his house the previous evening. The secondary assumption was that Daniel would be so prematurely embarrassed by the possibility of disclosing any details of our mutually shed virginities that he would confirm my whereabouts, yes, and then promptly change the subject completely. It might be crass to talk about them both as pawns, but I suppose I was just that confident about the moves that they would make.

I was mostly indifferent about their conversational preamble, and instead found myself distracted, studying Daniel from this new view. He rubbed at the back of his neck with such vigour that the muscles in both his forearm and upper arm flexed. I wondered then whether his body shared the aches that my own felt that afternoon. At the sound of my name – 'Sorry, Mrs Thompson, is Gillian actually home?' – my attention snapped back around as Daniel tried to steer the conversation. From my vantage point I could see both of them clearly enough, so I held my tongue and watched my plans for an alibi come together.

My mother laid her foundations masterfully. Yes, she told him, I was at home, resting, she thought, given that I was still hidden away upstairs, and I'd slept in much later than usual, so perhaps I'd had a poor night's sleep.

'I'd assumed that she'd be staying at yours when she didn't come home,' she said, a question without a question that saw Daniel's face immediately redden into a blush that stretched around near his ears.

'She did.' Daniel spat out the confirmation so abruptly that even I thought my mother was right to look so taken aback by his tone. It seemed that the longer I watched Daniel, the harder I had to fight to blink away images of the boy who I had left him for the previous evening.

When he spoke again his tone had softened. 'She did have a restless night, I mean. I think she just decided that she'd be more comfortable here in the end.'

My mother, lips thinned and arms folded, gave a careful nod before pushing forward with another question.

'Nothing happened, then?'

'I'm sorry?' Daniel hurried the words out in a much higher octave than usual.

He irregularly bounced on the balls of his feet and as I observed him, something both inconvenient and potentially problematic occurred to me: Daniel looked guilty. And from the expression that my mother wore in response to his outburst – one eyebrow arched, arms still firmly folded, a twist in her mouth that suggested she already didn't believe whatever Daniel was about to say – I was certain that she had noticed this as well.

'You two didn't have a fall-out?' she offered.

'Oh.' Daniel's shoulder dropped and his face gave way to a smile. 'Nothing like that, no. The opposite, if anything; we had a really lovely evening together. That daughter of yours is something special.'

I heard my mother's non-committal – and frankly a little hurtful – 'Hm' as I padded back towards my bedroom. I tamed my hair into an over-stretched bobble, pulled on a too-rigid pair of jeans that hadn't yet loosened following their latest wash, and seconds later I made a noisy display of walking down the stairs. The conversation instantly came to a halt when they saw me. My mother eyed me then, with an embarrassingly fake smile clawing at her mouth, while Daniel, by accident I assumed, dropped a small and nervous laugh in the hallway as he kneaded at the back of his neck.

'Do you want a cup of tea, Daniel?' my mother asked, lazily looking for something to fill the silence that I had created.

'I'm fine, thank you, Mrs Thompson.'

My mother nodded, smiled, and excused herself, leaving Daniel and me to float awkwardly around the open front door, apparently half-clueless as to how to properly behave around each other now. We had torn pieces from each other the previous evening, but now there was a ball of nervous energy wedged between us.

I tried to find something worth saying but my mind was a jumble of snapshot images now. I remembered how his breath had fallen out of him in great pants, from a mouth contorted into such a twist that under different circumstances it would have looked like he was in pain. I remembered slowing asking if he was okay. I couldn't remember why I'd done that. I couldn't remember my reasoning but I remembered his answer: 'I just want this to be good for you.'

The audio had the wrong image attached. It was Daniel's voice, but the boy's body, and my thrust, and although I shook it away there it was again immediately after until I

couldn't pull the individual components away from each other and I–

'Gillian?' Daniel set his hand on my shoulder, pulling me out of the memory – memories.

'Everything okay? You looked like you slipped out on me there.'

'Sorry.' I paused, shook away the last of the boy's face. 'I'm fine.'

He nodded, pressed his lips together, and then said: 'So how was it for you?' He laughed at the question, but the humour mostly escaped me, given that I thought we'd already half-had this conversation. My expression remained blank and so Daniel readjusted his tone when he spoke again, adding: 'Seriously, GT, was it okay?'

The house phone ringing cut through my thoughts then, but this was quickly extinguished by my mother answering the call from elsewhere in the house.

'It was mind-blowing,' I said.

But after that we fell into a game of reassurances. Every compliment that I delivered was met with a 'Really?' or a 'Do you mean that?' from Daniel, and I quite quickly ran out of ways to tell him how satisfactory his performance had been. He may have sensed this, or perhaps he just realised how one-sided our exchange of compliments had been. Whichever it was, something happened that made him move towards me then, the fingers of his right hand loose around my shoulders and his lips firm against my forehead.

He'd barely pulled away from this kiss when he muttered against my skin: 'You're a phenomenal woman, Gillian Thompson.'

'I am?'

'You are.'

'Gillian?'

I hadn't heard my mother step back into the hallway. She set the phone back in its cradle on the sideboard, prompting a musical tone from the handset to signal its charging.

'I've got to pop out, Gillian.'

Her face was pale, pained.

'Is everything okay, Mum?'

'Multiple stab wounds. Christ, he was only seventeen.'

I threw a puzzled expression at Daniel that he bounced back to me.

'Timothy Westburn.'

So that was his name then, I remember thinking. My mother had said it with some familiarity, and she looked at me with an expectant expression, waiting for a reaction. I nodded slowly, making a silent bid for more information.

'Anne's son?'

Daniel's hand was on my shoulder again now, delivering what I thought was meant to be a reassuring squeeze, but I still couldn't find a reaction for all of this.

'You'd know her by sight, Gillian; she's one of the women who brought food over, after your father.' She added this last bit with hesitation. And suddenly I knew exactly who my mother was referring to. Big hair, painful smile, workaholic husband, generic son.

Dead son now. Thanks to me.

Chapter twenty-seven

It had been eight days since Timothy Westburn's murder. Or the Westburn boy's murder, as our neighbours were now referring to it, which they did, multiple times, during any given conversation, whether it was relevant or not. No matter how tenuous the link, the women of our street would somehow find a way to incorporate the incident into their day-to-day chatter and the habit was apparently contagious given that within two days of the incident happening, my mother was suddenly suffering from this same affliction. Anne, a woman who we had never spoken to prior to my father's death, was suddenly the only person worth talking about and my mother, for reasons I couldn't fathom at the time, couldn't help but talk about her relentlessly. About her pain, and her loss, and about how horrible life must seem now. Each platitude was a knife to the stomach – for want of a better turn of phrase – although with hindsight I think that my mother might have known that, or at the very least hoped it.

'Doesn't it break your heart, Gillian?' she had asked once, in such a deadpan and unemotional tone that I had to watch her expression for a beat just to ascertain whether her question was serious.

'Of course it does, Mum.'

I saw her once. Anne Westburn, that is, not my mother. She was smuggled into the back of what I later thought must have been an unmarked police car. Even though she'd been staring out of the window, her resting expression suggested that she couldn't see a thing. My initial reaction, after that first contact, was unexpected and unstoppable, but then vomiting usually is. I pounded up the stairs as my glottis closed and my larynx raised, already anticipating the contraction of my diaphragm and the vigorous tensing of my abdominal walls. The biological procedure was a relatively familiar one. The shakes and sweating that followed were easily explained, as was the sudden feeling of dehydration. I could rationalise the whole act away as a biological reflux, a physical reaction, as it were. But I couldn't – or perhaps, didn't want to – explain, specifically, what it was a reaction to.

'Are you okay?' my mother asked from the doorway of the bathroom. I was perched on the closed toilet seat, leaning over the sink to cup handfuls of water into my mouth. Between gulps I replied: 'Probably a reaction to something.'

'Something that you've eaten?'

'What else would it be?' I snapped, already knowing, before the sentence was fully formed, that I shouldn't have done.

My mother was still asking too many questions. We discussed the Timothy

Westburn incident, at length, at the most inappropriate of times as well – over dinner, just before bed, sometimes even in Daniel's company – but we also discussed Daniel and me, how things were going, what the status of my feelings were, both in and outside the context of my newfound romantic relationship. And she appeared to pick over my answers with an attention that felt forensic in her hunt for minor details. Four days into the phenomenon of my mother talking over everything to within an inch of its life, even Daniel felt moved to extend a hypothesis on the matter.

'Do you think your mum knows?' He asked the question in a tone that made him sound only half-interested as we wandered through the aisles of Tesco.

These excursions to the supermarket had felt more natural – more normal – since I had lost touch with Paul. I'd only seen him once since the night it all happened, and even then it had been by coincidence, not design. Daniel had asked if we could be outside, go for a walk: 'What about that park you like?' The space meant something different now. Paul was no longer my immediate thought when the park was mentioned. I was even surprised when

I saw him that afternoon, with Peaches – and a different woman. By then I'd started to feel grateful that it hadn't been him after all.

'Gillian?'

Daniel's question caught me midway through picking out vegetables for dinner. 'Do you think she knows what?'

He let out a sharp breath. 'You know what, GT.'

Daniel paced away then, now appearing uninterested in the conversation he'd started.

'Christ, Daniel, how would she possibly know that?'

The words were hurried out, louder than intended, reaching Daniel, who was only five steps away now, and apparently catching one or two fellow shoppers on the way. A man and a woman – another couple, perhaps – turned, widened their eyes, and looked from me, the source of the noise, to Daniel, the equally startled target of it. Daniel laughed it off but as he moved over to me the couple promptly removed themselves from the aisle. He stood next to me, one arm wrapped around my shoulders with his chin balanced on my head as he made a gentle and entirely unwelcome 'Shh' sound.

'Hey, where did that come from?' he asked, pulling away to look down at me. I couldn't explain it away and so opted for a stern silence. Daniel leaned in and kissed my forehead. 'Sorry, GT, I'm sure she doesn't know. Like you said, how could she, right? How could anyone?'

***

Another four days rolled by without any anomalies occurring. I had recovered from the brief bout of vomiting and my digestive tract seemed to be in fully working order, but the choking sensation I experienced when Daniel and I rounded the corner to my street, to find a police vehicle parked directly outside my house, was undeniable. Daniel asked what they could be doing there; I don't think that I answered. The sound of chatter emanating from the living room instantly ceased as we closed the front door behind us and my mother appeared in the hallway soon after.

'There are some policemen here, Gillian.'

Hot Fuzz. 2007. Simon Pegg. 'She is not a policewoman. She's a police officer. Being a woman has nothing to do with it.'

I didn't correct her, although I desperately wanted to.

'They've asked if they can talk to you,' she added.

'Of course. That's fine,' I said, wondering whether I was actually allowed to refuse.

Inside the living room, perched side by side on the sofa, there were two men. One – the older one of the two – wore police constable attire. From what I could see of his white shirt, half-hidden beneath a black vest, his upper half was pressed with military precision, as were the trousers that completed him. He was leaning forward, forearms balanced on his knees and his hands hanging loose between them. When I glanced at his posture I noticed a wedding band. The notably younger model who sat alongside him boasted no signs of being married, but I had to wait until he lifted a hand to readjust his glasses to be sure. This other man was clearly the senior officer of the two – I've seen enough police dramas to know the difference in rank between a uniform and a suit. But his alleged seniority worried me slightly, partly due to his age but chiefly due to his fast and loose interpretation of what he must have considered to be appropriate work attire, which had left him looking too dishevelled for me to take seriously. The grey scuff mark at the front of his left shoe irked me. This second officer half-stood as my mother guided me into the room; he leaned over the coffee table to offer a handshake.

'Detective Sergeant Ayleson, and this is Police Constable Shiefs.'

'Pleased to meet you,' I said, instantly feeling that it wasn't right.

Both officers waited for me to position myself comfortably in the seat opposite them before they launched into their questions.

'Miss Thompson, on the night of the Timothy Westburn incident, did you see anyone unusual hanging around the street? Perhaps someone who you didn't recognise?' DS Ayleson fired off the question while his colleague remained stern alongside him, a pen already hovering over a small notebook, should I say anything at all worth writing down.

'I wasn't actually here much on the evening that it happened.'

'Oh, so you were where?'

'At a friend's house.' I flinched. I had used the wrong word. 'Boyfriend, sorry. At a boyfriend's house. My boyfriend.' I was suddenly conscious of Daniel, somewhere in the house, perhaps even directly outside of this room, listening to me fumble about with his title.

'Okay, and–'

'I came home,' I interrupted him, not knowing why I was offering this information so freely, yet instantly appreciating the world of difficulty it may open.

'During the night?'

'Yes.'

'And did you drive? Walk?'

'I walked, yes.'

PC Shiefs was writing something down. I had to physically restrain myself from taking the pen away from him.

'Whereabouts was that from?'

'He lives on Clevehill Close.'

'That's quite a walk back from there to here,' PC Shiefs chimed in at last.

'I like walking,' I replied, uncomfortably aware of how feeble the response sounded.

Detective Sergeant Ayleson picked up again then: 'Which way did you walk home?'

'I cut through the Coleman Estate and came along Neathfield Avenue.'

There was a flicker of something in Ayleson's face before he said: 'Isn't that the long way home?'

'It seemed safer to cut through the houses at that time of the night.'

'Safer, Miss Thompson? Why's that?'

'Given what was happening half an hour away in the other direction?'

'Although, you didn't know that at the time.'

'In hindsight,' I said and he nodded.

'Now, Miss Thompson, this boyfriend you mentioned—'

Daniel must have taken this as a cue. He appeared in the doorway then, slumped against the frame with an ease that suggested he had been perched there for the entire conversation. He raised a hand, as though replying to a roll call, and flashed a confident grin at the officers.

'Boyfriend,' he said.

They took what they must have considered to be the necessary details from Daniel then. His full name, his age, his address, the details of anyone living at home with him – a line of questioning they surely regretted taking – and they enquired about his relationship with me. It made for uncomfortable listening. Daniel was now sitting on the arm of the chair that I had tucked myself into, meaning there was no escaping his answers. Their words were swapped like trading cards over the top of me, as if I were just an aside now. As if Daniel had suddenly become the real star of the conversation. I resented that more than I should have done. But the conversation pulled back around and I brushed off that resentment, replacing it with what I believe was my first flutter of real panic since this interview ordeal had started.

'And what time did Miss Thompson leave your house?'

I felt Daniel shrug. When I looked up I found both officers looking to me for an answer then and I suddenly wondered where my mother was, whether she was within earshot, whether she would recognise a lie.

'I'm not sure what time I left, to be honest,' I offered. 'My mother heard me come home, so you might be best off asking her. I know it was quite early in the morning by the time I was getting into bed here.'

I left my answer deliberately vague, hoping to leave the officers without concrete facts to fall back on. The whole thing had felt remarkably similar to telling the truth. But then this was a version of the truth, I thought. This was the version of events that the majority knew now. And I wondered, idly – already knowing that it didn't, of course – whether that somehow made this the new truth.

'Verify that with the mother,' Ayleson said to Shiefs before flicking his eyes back in my direction. 'Miss Thompson, how old are you?'

'Twenty-two.'

'And you've lived here your whole life?'

'Not this house, but this area, yes.'

'And have you ever heard about any trouble in the area?'

Daniel and I exchanged quizzical looks. The question hadn't been directed at him but I had hoped that he could help me decipher it.

'Trouble?' Daniel pushed.

'Drugs, scraps, any issues with the younger members of this street, or the surrounding streets, that should have been mentioned to the police but maybe weren't, for one reason or another. Anything ringing a bell there?'

The more he developed the question, the less sure I felt about what he was actually asking me. 'No, no bells.' I said, weakly.

He sighed and so I assumed I must have given him the wrong answer. 'Timothy Westburn's murder has raised some serious questions for us here about youth groups in the area, Miss Thompson. I know you're a little older than the victim, but anything that you can think of now would be useful in our investigation into this.'

I had to hold back a smile. They had nothing. Absolutely nothing. And they were asking people – they were asking me, of all people – to try and help them. It was just beautiful, really. The whole situation was suddenly beautiful.

Obviously I knew nothing in that vein and I told them so. With Daniel's hand offering an unnecessarily reassuring squeeze on my shoulder, I explained to the two officers that I had never been considered popular enough to be drawn into that side of youth culture and they nodded, as if they knew something about that.

'I understand that, Miss Thompson,' DS Ayleson offered. But he couldn't. He was far too attractive, far too likeable, to possibly understand. DS Ayleson struck me as the sort of person who was simply given his normalcy at birth; some of us had to work for ours. 'In which case, I think we're about finished here for the time being. Thank you, both,' he said, as if he'd suddenly remembered that Daniel had appeared midway through the process. The four of us exchanged pleasantries ahead of our collective goodbye. DS Ayleson offered me his business card on the understanding that I would contact him should I remember anything that would be useful.

What, like my having killed the boy? A voice offered from somewhere in the rear of my cranium and on hearing it I wondered where my guilt was now.

'Thank you again for your time,' the senior officer said on his way out of the front door, taking with him little to no information, and concluding my first and, as it turned out, final, encounter with the police.

Chapter twenty-eight

It was one week and six days on from my audience with the police when my mother found me in my bedroom, neatly folding items of clothing into squares that were then stacked regimentally on top of each other in properly marked boxes. The clothing I had worn on that night was the first to be packed, tucked away beneath a winter wardrobe that I wouldn't need for another three months. There were two weeks remaining of the summer holiday from university, and I was eager to get back to the normalcy of that life. The daily experiments, the forced conversations with people whose names I barely remembered, because they hardly required or even wanted me to. There was a feeling of familiarity with your fellow students and simultaneous anonymity in your surroundings, which made university life markedly easier than the life I had been trying to piece together at home.

'You aren't due back for weeks yet,' my mother said, arms folded as she leaned against the doorframe.

Somewhere between her saying this and my finding a reply she moved over to my bed and sat down rigidly on the mattress.

'You can never be too prepared, Mum. You taught me that.'

'I'm glad that I managed to teach you something.'

The words were chased out by a sigh as she began to survey the room around her.

'You've taught me lots of things, Mum.'

'Mm, like what?'

I hadn't been anticipating this. She eyed me for an uncomfortably long time and I suddenly became all too aware of how hot my face felt. I fumbled, searching for anything now.

'You taught me how to tie my shoes, didn't you?'

She may have done. But I had a nagging feeling that it had been my grandfather from my father's side who had actually done that for me.

'Yes, Gillian, I did,' she said, with a tint of amusement colouring her words. 'Not much of a legacy, is it, as mother-daughter bonding goes? Shoe tying and preparedness.'

'They haven't made any developments, have they, about the Timothy Westburn murder?' She changed the topic without skipping a beat and it unnerved me. I was sure she had put a heavy emphasis on murder, but felt unsure of why. 'Have you heard anything about it?' she continued.

'Why would I have done?' I snapped, the words sounding sharper than I had meant them to. I knew my mother would have noticed. I continued packing as I waited for her response, my eyes firmly averted.

'The police seemed to think that you might have.'

I dropped what I was holding. I can't even tell you what it was, but I distinctly recall trying to make the action look deliberate.

Everything that my mother said during the opening stretch of that conversation felt like a double entendre. But the indecent and amusing second meaning had been replaced by something accusatory and unsettling. Unsure of how to proceed, I blindly felt my way about the conversation that followed, breathing a sincere sigh of relief when my mother changed the subject to something I felt more able to discuss adequately.

'How are things going with Daniel?'

My stomach lurched. I had become accustomed to the feeling.

'Things are going well, I think, thank you.' *Should I offer more information?* I remember thinking. When my mother failed to pick the conversation up, I decided that yes, I probably should. 'We've been discussing what will happen when I'm back at university, actually.'

Two evenings prior to this Daniel had launched the conversation. We had just finished dinner and we were in the midst of tidying away cooking utensils when he said: 'I'm going to miss you.'

I turned, tea towel in hand and a puzzled expression on my face. 'When?'

'When you go back to university, idiot.'

'Oh.'

Daniel shuffled slightly, apparently waiting for something.

'Do you…' he started, paused, swallowed. Tried again. 'Do you think that you'll miss me, or – that's dumb, right?'

We hadn't decided precisely what would happen when I returned to university but we had decided that we would attempt to stay together. As I repeated this conversation to my mother she raised her eyebrows at this but, again unsure of the meaning behind the expression, I pressed on with my retelling of the transcript. 'Daniel mentioned moving to Bristol with me but I'm not sure that's a good idea.'

'Why not?'

Because then he would find out what I am, surely, I thought.

'Because it all seems very fast,' I said instead.

My mother nodded, her eyes narrowed as though inspecting my expression for a nervous tick, or a tell.

Our conversation continued in this vein as we leisurely wandered around the topic of Daniel, my relationship with him, and my plans to pursue that further. Still feeling about blindly, I was at least by now half-confident that I had constructed a convincing and reliable narrative to stretch out for the remainder of the conversation. But as the minutes rolled into a half-an-hour block of time, I realised that we would soon run out of Daniel-related chatter. My mother, though, had planned ahead. She had already decided what we would discuss next. Before I could find another foundation on which to steady a conversation, my mother, with an unexpected air of confidence, looked me in the eye and said: 'And does Daniel know what he's actually given you an alibi for, or have you managed to keep that from him so far?'

I would love to give you details of the blind panic that followed; of the sensation of my mother's words tickling at my amygdaloid nucleus, and how my brain promptly smashed neurotransmitters together by way of a response. But all I loosely remember from the seconds that came immediately after this well-crafted revelation was a distinct feeling of 'Hm, so my mother knows', as if she'd caught a younger me smoking outside a friend's house, or engaging in sexual activities before my time. 'Hm, so my mother knows' was the best that my above-average mind could settle on.

'You'll have to say something eventually, Gillian.'

She was too calm, too measured. This perturbed me more than the question itself had.

'How are you so calm?' I asked, leaning forward. I needed to see her face.

'I've had a lot of time to think about this.'

'How much time? I mean, how long have you thought this?' I chose my words with care; I couldn't – wouldn't – admit to anything, not yet.

My mother, her eyes closed now, mouthed illegible words and bounced her head lightly, presumably in time with her thoughts, as though she were attempting to give me an exact temporal measurement.

'I've thought it since the police visited,' she said, still in a measured tone. 'Daniel doesn't know when you left the house that night – he's guessing. The shower drain was caked with something the morning after that boy died. I just didn't know what it was. It's clear what you and Daniel have been up to, so I thought, or I might have hoped, that it was something to do with that. But the bloody clothes hidden in your wardrobe gave me a better idea.' Even through all of this my mother remained calm, on an intimidating level, and for the first time I entertained the possibility that perhaps not all of my psychological quirks had come from my father. 'And let's not forget the fact that you haven't actually denied it,' she concluded.

But I haven't admitted to it either, I thought.

'A normal person would have denied it, Gillian.' She paused and exhaled hard in an almost-laugh. 'But then, a normal person wouldn't have killed someone.'

Forrest Gump. 1994. Sally Field. 'What does normal mean, anyway?'

Halloweentown. 1998. Debbie Reynolds. 'Being normal is vastly overrated.'

Carrie. 2013. Chloë Grace Moretz. 'I want to be normal.'

'Gillian?'

'I'm trying to find something to say.'

She let out another hard sigh. 'I think anything would be good at this point, love.'

'Are you going to tell anyone about this?' I wasn't sure whether this was an acceptable starting point, morally speaking, but it seemed like a logical one.

My mother clearly had a plan – she had been sitting on this information for long enough to have developed a fairly detailed one – and I needed to know what my role in it would be. She let out a noise that would have been considered a sharp laugh, under different circumstances, and I thought then that perhaps she hadn't meant it when she said anything would be a good thing to say.

'I understand why you might feel disappointed in me, Gillian,' she said. I thought this was a peculiar place to start. 'I haven't been good at all, especially not recently.'

'Why would I be disappointed in you, Mum?'

I was sure that it should be the other way around. I was standing in front of her then, meaning I caught the narrow-eyed glance that she threw in my direction like I had just asked something stupid of her.

She went back to avoiding eye contact before speaking again. 'You are always meant to love your children.' She spoke as if that were a complete explanation, but then added: 'I know there must have been times when it seemed like I didn't.'

I nodded, although I didn't feel like she'd answered my question.

She started again. 'Your father and I did this. You have to take responsibility, Gillian, of course. But we did this as well. I sometimes wonder whether you ever stood a chance with us.'

I marvelled at her level tone, her measured presentation, as though reading each snippet from an autocue positioned somewhere beyond my bedroom.

'You saw all of that violence for years. And it fed something.'

My mother continued in this vein for longer than felt necessary, feeding snippets of my childhood to the case-hungry nature-versus-nurture debate, which my mother sat firmly in the centre of during her soliloquy. She shifted between believing there was something wrong with me and believing there was something wrong with my life, and she almost made a good case, I remember thinking. But it's hard to be definitive one way or another with these things without a formal diagnosis of the participant in question – in this case, me.

'I don't think bringing Daniel into this is fair either, Gillian,' she said, shifting topics.

Analyze This. 1999. Robert De Niro. 'What, are you gonna start moralizing on me?'

I swallowed the quote. I knew that I couldn't take that tone with her. I stood in front of her then, waiting for another nugget of something to fall from her mouth. With my hands tucked behind my back, I was a child waiting for their reprimand from a troubled parent. *I'm sorry I stole the cookie, Mum. I'm sorry I killed the boy*. My idle apologies may have worked when I was younger, but I felt I should keep them to myself now.

'What if he finds out?' she pushed.

'He won't,' I snapped out, instantly realising how defensive I sounded.

'I did.'

'You're different.'

'Because I'm your mother?'

'Yes.' I considered for a beat longer. 'Because you're my mother, you're different.'

She rubbed at her eyes and sighed then. A heavy, exhausted, emotional sigh. 'Why, Gillian? Why him?'

I remembered the footsteps, how the boy had been running towards me, and how, for a split second as he lay there, I thought that this could be self-defence. But that argument required reasonable force, which I suspected would be misplaced in a case of an armed versus unarmed individual. I could have called someone, though, I thought to myself then, not for the first time since it had happened. I could have called someone and I truly believed – or had to believe – that when I left to call for help, that was my honest intention. But I've heard the road to hell is paved with the best of those. And an honest intention doesn't count for much at all when you have a knife buried to the hilt in someone's abdomen.

'Because he was there,' I said eventually, somewhat ashamedly, giving her the most honest answer that I could lay my hands on.

My mother didn't speak for a while after that. I didn't think to count how long, exactly, but it was definitely longer than a minute. I shuffled, I moved forward, only to move back to my original position seconds later, and I even tried to speak, just once, only for the first syllable to be met with a headshake from my mother who was now staring determinedly at the floor. When she did speak the sentiment was simple but the voice that uttered it sounded newly vulnerable: 'I will protect you.'

She paused to pull in a large mouthful of air, fuelling whatever was going to come from her next. 'You won't understand this until you have children, you know, Gillian. You'll know that I'm doing this because I'm your mother but you'll never understand. Not really.' She spoke more to the floor than she did to me. 'It will kill me as much as it killed that poor boy, Christ, and his poor mother.' She paused for a shaky breath, stifling a sob. 'It will kill me, but you are my daughter and… I can't. I can't do that. I won't.'

Dexter. 2006. James Remar. 'Remember this forever – you are my son, you are not alone, and you are loved.'

I sighed heavily and on hearing this sign of relief my mother picked up again: 'But it needs to stop, Gillian. This whole bloody nightmare needs to stop.'

And what if it doesn't? I wanted to ask her. Her eyes snapped up at me as though I had said the query aloud. She stood up from the bed and stared at me with a determination that I had never seen my mother wear before.

'I won't do this for you again. If it doesn't stop, then you're on your own.' And she left, pulling my bedroom door closed behind her.

Chapter twenty-nine

The thought that perhaps my mother was in part responsible – more responsible than she would ever admit, at least – for the less than savoury elements of my psychopathic make-up occurred with more frequency in the days that followed her big reveal. We spoke as normal from the morning after the event, and she addressed me with such ease that the whole thing felt almost anti-climactic. As though in the absence of explosions, accusations, and snide remarks, I was somehow now desperate for them. I had been intermittently reprimanded for various behaviours my entire life, and yet, somehow, the comeuppance for this one fell short of my expectations of how a normal mother should react. If indeed there is a normal reaction to discovering that your child is now a murderer.

'How are you doing this?' I finally asked her, in response to a question about whether I would be home for dinner or not.

'Cooking?'

'No, being so normal.'

She sighed. 'Would you prefer me to outwardly hate you, Gillian?'

I tried to decipher whether there was an implication that she now inwardly hated me.

'We've discussed it. I don't want to spend the rest of our lives discussing it because frankly if we do then there's every possibility that I'll change my mind about what we're doing here.' She said the words with confidence, as if this were another normal conversational exchange to take part in while putting away the weekly shopping. 'If you need to discuss it, genuinely need to, then we can, but I'd rather we didn't, starting now.' She slammed a kitchen cupboard closed, punctuating her point. 'Now, are you home for dinner or not?'

When I left the house thirty minutes later my mother didn't even ask where I was going. She assumed that it was to Daniel's, I suppose. A safe assumption to make on a normal day, but there was another man who required my attention that morning. I stopped en route to buy twelve yellow roses, and then I walked to meet him. The journey took less time than I had originally calculated, and before I'd had time to put together my perfect opener, I was in front of him, placing the flowers on the ground, and pinching at the knees of my trousers to loosen them before kneeling down.

'Morning, Dad.'

I reached out my fingertips towards the headstone in front of me and traced the letters one by one.

In Loving Memory Of
Joseph Thompson
Beloved Husband, Father and Friend

The longer I stared at the words the more I had to concentrate on stifling a small laugh. 'That must have been written by a stranger. Unless she really does have a sense of humour after all.'

I slapped the top of the headstone with the same vigour that my father had always used when punching my shoulder, usually when he had made a joke at my mother's expense. 'But you can't be offended by a joke, so s'alright,' I could hear him spitting into my ear.

Half-sitting on my father's bones now, I pushed the flowers a little closer to the headstone.

'I bought you these, out of politeness, really.'

The surrounding graves were littered with fresh flowers and sentimental trinkets; there were cards, laminated photographs, overwhelming markers of love and grief that I played voyeur to for a moment, before turning back to the headstone in front of me. My father's grave had gone unacknowledged since the afternoon that he had been flung into it.

'You'll remember all about keeping up appearances, won't you?'

I ran my palm flat across the face of the grave, brushing away small chunks of debris that had managed to attach themselves.

'Maybe I should have come sooner, but I didn't really know what I could say. I still don't. Maybe I should apologise to you, but then…' I shook the idea from my head. 'You'd know that I didn't mean it.'

My hands dropped into my lap and I leaned back from the stone, putting an additional two inches between us. There was no rush, I reassured myself; I had ample time to decipher what I could and shouldn't say. I heard Louise then, her coo of reassurance, her 'This is a safe space, Gillian, there are no shoulds here – try and remember that.' She was right, of course: this was a safe space now.

'You're about the only person I can be honest with, I suppose,' I said, noting how dejected I sounded by the admission.

A rustle of grass somewhere behind me bought me an additional minute of thinking time while one grieving relative tended to a dead one. From this angle, they probably thought that I was praying. When the silence had settled again I took a cautious glance around to verify that we really were alone. While I still hadn't decided what I was about to divulge, I was sure that it wasn't something that I would want anyone to overhear.

'You've missed a lot,' I started.

I told him about Daniel, Mum, Emily. I span out the sordid tale of Emily, her request that Daniel help her to end her life and his eventual compliance with that. I explained the closeness – the need for closeness – with Daniel following his confession, and how what I had done to Timothy – what I had needed to do – had somehow become inextricably bound up in those feelings of closeness, like opening myself up to one set of emotions had made me vulnerable to experiencing others. One feeling leading to another seemed like a normal emotional reaction for a normal girl, just that one time. But a small laugh escaped me as I tried to squeeze into the label. If I listened carefully then I could catch my father's curt 'HA!' as he joined in with the joke.

This was the first opportunity that I'd had for such an uninhibited confession of feelings. I was all too aware of the bitter twist of irony cutting through it though: this outpouring, to my father no less. The first man I had known, loved, hurt – killed. Now I was talking to him like he was someone I trusted. I reached forward and ran my fingers over the lies hammered into his headstone. Palm flat against the surface, as though needing physical support, I confessed: 'I think that there's something wrong with Mum.'

Psycho. 1960. Anthony Perkins. 'Mother – what's the phrase? She isn't quite herself today.'

'She's completely herself,' I explained. 'And I feel like she shouldn't be.' I relayed the last four days to my father; how my mother had helped me pack, cooked me meals, even offered to take me shopping – although shopping for what exactly, she couldn't say: 'I don't know, Gillian, anything you might need.' There were moments when I had felt that she was the one making up for something, while I felt confident that it should have been the other way around. 'Mum thinks that you and she has something to do with what I did, said I never stood a chance, that you'd worked together to breed a little monster.' A small laugh broke through; not quite the real live girl I had been hoping to portray. 'She obviously thinks that you and I are quite similar in a lot of ways too.' I paused here, noting how uncomfortable the thought was. 'Funny, really, when it's you and her who share similarities at the moment. You've both kept secrets for me now.' I wondered whether my father would have kept this secret – and an unwelcome thought appeared then: could I really trust my mother to? I thought of her bustling about the kitchen, refusing to discuss what had happened.

'Do you think I can trust her?'

My mind flicked to an image of my mother, hiding her best carving knives, asking herself a similar question. Maybe my mother and I weren't that dissimilar after all.

'She might think it still, but I'm nothing like you. I could never hurt her, or him. I'd hurt someone else first, always.' I said the words boastfully, although I'm unsure now why I felt such pride. 'And they'll both protect me. That's what I know now; that's what I can really take away from all of this.'

I pressed my knuckles against the ground to help lever myself into a standing position. My knees were caked with damp mud that I tried to brush away before it had time to dry into the fabric.

'Like I said before, you and I are different types of monsters.' I leaned hard on the top of the stone. 'You were an animal. You just couldn't help yourself; I know that now. And I know that I'll do this much better than you did. I can be better, kinder, normal. I can be a real person; Daniel will make me that.'

I ran my muddied hand over the top of the headstone and took a step closer to him; bending over at the waist, I lowered myself down until my lips were nearly touching the granite. When I inhaled against it I was overwhelmed by the blend of warm lager and raw meat that had always come home from work with him. I lowered my voice down to a whisper level before saying my goodbye.

'In case you were wondering, Dad, I don't regret you at all.'

I pressed my lips down on the stone, planting an abrupt kiss on its surface.

Now

It is Monday now, which means two things: I have a late seminar at university, and it is Daniel's day to cook dinner. A month after Daniel moved in with me – four months after I moved back to Bristol – he pinned a cleaning and cooking rota to the door of my fridge, and we have mostly adhered to the timetable. When I return home carrying double the number of textbooks that I left the house with in the morning, Daniel is already busying himself in the kitchen. It isn't until I thump the deadweight of academic literature down on our dining table that he even seems to notice that I've walked into the room.

'Christ, GT, drop those any louder?' he says, reaching out to turn down the radio before turning to look at me. 'You could scare the hair off a cat.'

I try to hold in a flicker of something – intrigue? – prompted by his analogy.

'Sorry, I didn't mean to make you jump.'

He waves away the apology and smiles before returning to the chopping board in front of him. The radio is turned down to an inaudible level but the voices create something like a hum in the background.

'What were you listening to?' I ask.

'This police panel show sort of thing. It wasn't great, to be honest, but they're talking about that kid – you know, the one who died round your area?'

I am jarred to hear Daniel's flippancy on this topic, but I have, deep down, been waiting for this to come up. We are closing in on a year since Timothy Westburn's murder and the police are yet to make an arrest for it – in fact, they are yet to even isolate a suspect. The closest they have come to something promising, something concrete, is a statement that was released six months after the incident.

'We're looking for a man in his mid to late thirties. Short dark hair, dark eyes, of average body build, approximately six foot two in height. We have a witness who has placed him at the scene of the crime and it is imperative that we contact him as this investigation moves forward.'

I couldn't remember seeing anyone who matched that description. Unlikely though it was, for a moment I wondered whether the police were desperate enough for a suspect that they would fabricate one entirely – but it was a poor effort, if that were the case. Not only were they looking for a make-believe monster, but their killer had been given the wrong height and build, not to mention genitalia.

'It's crazy though, right?' Daniel says, pulling me back into the kitchen where he is now lifting a casserole dish into the open oven. I have hated casseroles since my father's death, which prompted repeated deliveries of them, miraculously deposited on mine and my mother's doorstep at seemingly random intervals. But it doesn't feel right to mention this to Daniel after six months of him cooking them and my feigning enjoyment at eating them. 'Don't you think?' Daniel picks up again, noting my extended silence.

'What's crazy?'

'That they never found that kid's killer.'

'I don't know. It happens, doesn't it? You hear about it more often these days.'

Daniel considers this for a moment. 'I still think it's mental, GT. Someone out there is a murderer and, like, no one has any idea. He's just walking around, living his life. Christ, he might even have family.'

He might even be a woman.

'Do you think anyone knows?' Daniel says, sounding more excited than I think he should.

I can't talk about this any longer, I decide, not without things tightening in my chest, not without breathing becoming a little uncomfortable. I walk over to him and, tiptoeing slightly, I kiss the side of his temple.

'I think you must have had a boring day at work to be so excited over this.'

Daniel laughs because he has learnt to take these comments light-heartedly, no matter how serious I appear when I say them. And given that he is working as a financial assistant again, boring is probably exactly what his day has been.

'Fair point,' he says, before kissing me back. 'Casserole okay for dinner?'

He turns and so can't see the twinge of a grimace that appears when he asks this. 'Perfect. How long will it be?'

'How long do you need?'

Daniel knows that there are nights when I need to escape for a while, and on these nights he thinks that I run. I am usually gone for anywhere up to an hour and while I do leave the house donning athletic attire, and I do return reasonably sweaty, the process isn't quite as simple as I have allowed Daniel to believe for the last six months.

'An hour?' I say, already knowing that this is fine and that, if necessary, Daniel will halt dinner preparations and pick them up again when I'm home.

'An hour is fine, GT, I've got some work to do anyway.' He is still chopping at something when I move to the leave the kitchen, but I halt when he throws a quick 'Love you' after me. Human or not, these moments still baffle me.

American Psycho. 2000. Christian Bale. 'And though I can hide my cold gaze, and you can shake my hand and feel flesh gripping yours and maybe you can even sense our lifestyles are probably comparable...... I simply am not there.'

'You too,' I say, already halfway out the door.

When I leave the flat I am wearing loose-fitting jogging bottoms and an ill-fitting T-shirt that used to belong to Daniel.

However, much like many of his other clothes, I have now adopted this too as part of my own wardrobe. I shout goodbye but he has already connected himself to a set of headphones that are wired into his laptop and so he doesn't hear me leave.

The run to the storage centre used to take me half an hour on its own. But, as with all exercise, I have become more accustomed to the run over time and it now takes little more than fifteen minutes. I exchange pleasantries with the guard at the entrance – 'How's the family?' I ask, as I do every time I walk through these gates – and head to my storage unit which is, as requested on initially signing the contract for it, one of the furthest from the main entrance. 'I'm particular about proximity,' I had said to the manager and he had shrugged, taken my money in exchange for the key and then disappeared, seemingly nonplussed by my request. Over the last ten months I have learnt that people are often too busy with their own unmentionables to go rummaging about in yours, unless they have a particularly good reason to.

'What's in storage, anyway?' Daniel had asked, after accidentally opening an invoice for the space.

'Boxes,' I had replied. 'University experiments, old clothes, you know.' And that had pacified him entirely.

Inside my unit – number 034 – there are in fact five boxes.

Experiments.

Miscellaneous.

DG.

AT.

And the most recent addition: PW.

When I arrive home a little over an hour later I am already drafting an apology to Daniel who, I assume, will be readying dinner. When I walk through the front door though, I can see that Daniel is sitting in the living room, his elbows perched on his knees and his eyes fixed on something that is moving across the television screen.

'Daniel?' I raise my voice a little, pretending that I haven't seen him.

'In here, GT.'

When I walk into the living room I can see that it is a news report that has Daniel so transfixed. I brace myself for another police panel, or worse still a commemorative speech from The Mother of the Boy, but instead Daniel cuts through the broadcast to announce: 'They found him.'

'Who?'

'That bloke. That Peter Whatshisname bloke.'

'Wincher,' I say.

'Yes, that's the bloke – that's the bloke they've found.' Daniel says this with a level of excitement that seems disproportionate for the announcement that he's making. 'You know the one who went missing last month? They've bloody found him.'

'Where?'

'His body was dumped at some running track or another. How they've only just found him, mind, on a track like that, I've got no idea.'

Probably because he was well hidden, I think, but I say nothing.

The interactions between the live feed and the studio fill our momentary silence.

'And what have the police said about this so far, Claire?' says the smart-looking middle-aged news anchor who is taking up the right half of our television screen.

'The police have said very little, Philip, but we have heard some speculation that Peter Wincher's case is markedly similar to those of David Green and Aaron Turner, which we saw earlier this year. The police, understandably so, don't want to encourage rumour,' the woman says, maintaining what feels like an intimidating level of eye contact with the camera. 'But there is talk of this being a killing spree of sorts, potentially at the hands of one individual.'

The X Files. 1997. Gillian Anderson. 'Psychologists often speak of the denial of an unthinkable evil… What we can't possibly imagine ourselves capable of we can blame on the ogre, on the hunchback, on the lowly half-breed.'

On the unnamed, inhuman individual.

I turn the television off.

'Why did you do that?' Daniel asks, irked by the interruption.

'Why do you want to watch that, Daniel? It's gutter press.'

'Gutter press? Gillian, there could be a bloody serial killer out there.'

'Oh, Daniel, don't be so absurd,' I snap, biting harder at him than I mean to and he is visibly pained by my tone. 'I'm sorry. It's just… it's scary, don't you think?'

Living with Daniel has been invaluable to my developing how to talk to people. We had been living together for just six weeks when I had perfected this tone – this meek and vulnerable tone – that led to him offering me comfort for one thing or another, and that's exactly what he does. Daniel stands from the sofa and wraps an arm around my shoulders. He plants a kiss near the crown of my head and says: 'Sorry, GT. I know how stuff like that gets to you.'

And it does get to me, in ways that Daniel will never understand.

'But hey, whoever it is that's bumping these folks off, you obviously don't need to worry,' he says, and I give him a quizzical look. 'Well, they're all blokes, aren't they?' He winks, and it is clear that he is trying to be playful, so I smile in return.

We both walk to the kitchen and while Daniel continues with his preparations for dinner, I fabricate details of my run – 'I really think I'm getting my time down now' – in the hope that this will keep Daniel busy. I am talking and talking at a frantic pace but somewhere in the back of my head I am already replaying things.

Replaying Daniel. And when he places our plates on the dining table, I hear him, clear as day.

'Someone out there is a murderer and, like, no one has any idea. She's just walking around, living her life. Christ, she might even have family.'

'You okay there, GT?' Daniel asks.

'Walking around, living my life, I'm doing okay,' I say, before I tuck into my casserole.

Acknowledgments

Intention was born in the Creative Writing department of the University of Birmingham in 2015. The PhD cohort were brutal but brilliant in their feedback, and the same can be said of my supervisors: Dan Vyleta and Ruth Gilligan. Thank you all for your help and support over the course of those three years; this book simply would not be the same without you.

There were a lot of other helping hands over those years too. I can't name names – we'd be here forever – but to the people who listened, or pretended to listen; to the people who didn't give me a stink-eye for explaining what Gillian gets up to in her free-time; to the people who put up with me saying over and over how I couldn't do it, and telling me over and over that I could:

Thank you, a million times over.

Lightning Source UK Ltd.
Milton Keynes UK
UKHW041314220119
335980UK00001B/24/P